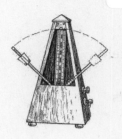

BRAND NEW BEAT

Gary Owen
Chelsea Villa,
27 Slater Avenue
Derby
DE1 1GT
TEL. 07816 322891

Also by Deborah Tyler-Bennett
from The King's England Press:

Poetry
Clark Gable in Mansfield
Revudeville
Napoleon Solo Biscuits
Mr Bowlly Regrets

Fiction
Turned Out Nice Again
Mice That Roared

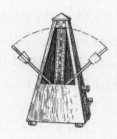

BRAND NEW BEAT

Swinging Short Fictions

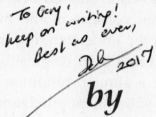

To Gary!
keep on writing!
best as ever,
Deb 2017

by

Deborah Tyler-Bennett

THE KING'S ENGLAND PRESS

2017

ISBN 978-1-909548-70-1

BRAND NEW BEAT
is typeset and published by
The King's England Press
111 Meltham Road
Lockwood
HUDDERSFIELD
West Riding of Yorkshire
HD4 7BG
© Deborah Tyler-Bennett, 2017

Printed and bound in Great Britain by
Lulu Press Inc. Digital Print on Demand.

**Once again, these stories
are for Dad, and in
memory of Mum.**

Acknowledgments: Thanks go to Martyn, for listening to first drafts of these stories, and my family for their support. Dad helped me with many of the 1960s details. Some of these stories were honed via suggestions from my creative writing students in Derby, Beeston, and Loughborough, thanks to them, particularly Celia Dolan who wrote me a list of drinks for the various pubs in the book, and Helena Joyce whose lovely memoir piece on the seaside reminded me of the incident from my family history that was the inspiration for 'Big Wheels'. Thanks to Denise Reidy, who advised on Police procedures for the stories on Norrie. Steve Rudd has, as always, shaped how the book came about. Thanks to Ian Blake, Sally Evans, and all at *Callander Poetry Weekend* for their inspiration. Thanks to Ross Bradshaw and all at *States of Independence* who hosted one of the first readings from the book. Also, Jack Strutt and the *Max Miller Appreciation Society* have been very supportive of the three books in this series. Not one of these pieces would have been written without the story-telling of my late Mum, Doris Tyler.

Historical Note: Although the *New Beat* tour in this book was partly inspired by the *Motown* tours of Britain in the 1960s, it's invented, as are the acts who take-part in it. Likewise, versions of real Brighton and Mansfield shops and pubs were played-with and re-imagined (sometimes even re-built) for the sake of fiction. By the 1960s, many variety performers and theatres were finding times increasingly tough, and some venues hosted bingo, film, or nude shows in-order to survive.

The story about the changeling is my version of an old English folk-tale. Amongst versions of the story is one in

Brian Froud and Alan Lee's *Faeries* (London: Pan, 1978) p.67. The poem extract Grandwem reads at Norrie's funeral is from E. V. Lucas's anthology *The Open Road* (Methuen, 1924) and is from Bliss Carman's popular poem 'The Joys of the Road,' p.19.

This book can be read as the third part of the trilogy that began with *Turned Out Nice Again*, and *Mice that Roared*, which saw the characters move from the 1940s to the 1950s, but can just as easily be read and enjoyed as a single volume.

Contents

THE HOME PRESERVATION SOCIETY

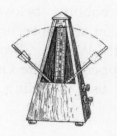

Mr Stringer's Favourite Dance

Alf considered Grandwem's dancing with Beryl and Shirl was both the funniest thing he'd ever seen and the most touching.

Not a current record, but an older one, *Hoots Mon* by Lord Rockingham's Eleven: must have been at least 'fifty-eight when that was first released.

"Da da da da

de da da da

de de da da de da da."

Thrusting carpet-slippers on parquet, stockings perilously close to rolling-down. "Dah dah dah..." Grandwem, and eventually George twisting and yelling with Shirl and Beryl: "there's a moose, loose, aboot this hoose."

Beryl, and Auntie Shirl spiralling happily, all fondant short skirts and sequinned dome-earrings. Grandwem in pinnie, turban, and George in his grey slacks and fair-isle tank top, shook as if there were an earth tremor. George's tank-top seeming in danger of unravelling by dint of pure effort.

Grandwem's face was oyster-tight, her gyrating as if life depended on it. "Dah Dah da."

13

There they went, bobbing below the sunburst wire-framed mirror Alf'd won after a record thirty-seven goes at *Crack That Crab* on the Wakes. Dancing as if they'd be guillotined if they stopped, despite Grandwem's green and yellow Murano glass fish wobbling fit to topple off the sideboard.

"Dah da da..."

"It's great fun, Alfred, why don't you stop being a reet stick-in-the-mud and join us?"

"Too much like hard work, Win."

"Please yoursen."

As they rocked with Lord Rockingham's, Beryl said: "How come my work in costume takes me to all those supper-clubs and posh places, and the best times I have are here in Mansfield, with you lot?"

Grandwem chortled: "That's easy, love, George and I have lived wi' so much cack and offal, we really know how to enjoy us sens."

"Aye, it's later than you think," George laughed.

So, they danced on, Beryl kicking and swivelling hips, pale lipstick glimmering like her earrings. And... She wouldn't tell them, not yet, as nowt was showing. But the truth had her closed-up, made her long to shout out like a Forest fan at a home match: "I met a boy in Slab Square by the Council House left lion, and he was about to meet a girl, but she never showed. And he waited and waited, and I was waiting too, for Sylvie Evans from the Royal's box office. Well, Sylvie didn't show, and his girl didn't either, and we ended-up talking. Just talking. I was only being friendly, and he seemed nice. So, we said we'd go for one at

The Bell, just so it wasn't a wasted evening. And we did, and three rum-and-blacks later he took me to a room at The Gresham and … and … well, bogger me, I'm up the stick, what did you want me to say?"

But Beryl was telling nothing like this version of events, which would have been both true and not any road. She knew, with her patent-white, London bought, shoes and matching handbag, she looked like a career girl. The bag was under George Formby, Grandwem's budgie's, cage, she could hear the bird happily dropping seed onto it.

George Formby – the budgie Grandwem kept replacing on the sly. This incarnation was harsher green than previous, and docker-gobbed. Quiet… all quiet… then: "Sod me, it's the fancy man!" Even though the war was long ended, Grandwem had still taught him to whistle: "Have a pint, Win, and bogger Hitler!"

"Ruder than ever,' thought Grandwem, hard-edged as a Nottingham factory girl on a Saturday Night, 'boggers' as groups of these were known, rampaging Slab Square, all lippy and promises. Those sprees were summat to behold, and no mistake. ARE OUR GIRLS BAD AS THE BOYS? *The Evening Post* had posed, showing a cover of a dark haired razor-boy, with a pouting, check-shirted girl. Young people had always got it in the neck from folk, thought Grandwem.

Yes, George Formby might be rude but, as far as Grandwem Win was concerned, he was the voice of her neighbourhood, and good luck to it.

In her heart of hearts, Grandwem had noted Beryl's swelling belly, and known what was up. Beryl was no spring chick anymore, and hadn't had a steady boy. There had been a few possibles, but as her job had demanded more of her, she'd kept love on a back-burner. "That girl's past her prime," old Mrs Dobbs down the road had said, "she's a jobbing old maid and no mistake. These days they want money and glamour, not husbands and kiddies, I've never heard the like."

"Din't we want owt like that? It just weren't available, then." Grandwem had put in.

"If you ask me, we were better off. Wi a man you tek charge, then you aren't disappointed."

Beryl's tummy was pushing her dress's fabric as she danced.

Who was the culprit?

Concentrate on the music…

Concentrate…

"Da da da da da de dah dah."

"That were a grand dance, put it on again."

Beryl looked at Grandwem, who was fixing her chicken-leg stockings back in place. Did she know? Alf often remarked that Grandwem knew all there was to know, and more besides. If you lied, she'd prize the truth out like a winkle on a cocktail-stick. She must know. "I don't want a baby, not ever, I love my work and I'm just on really good money. Soon, I could be costuming whole shows myself, I've worked years for it. But I'm so stupid, I might as well have not done anything and stayed at home."

She thought of coming home, and staring admiringly at friends' babies whilst thinking "Glad it's not me." What had she been thinking that night at the left lion?

Alf watched them dance, a bit slower this time. "I'm done." Said George, seeking the formica table and sitting at it: "Bring us one of them Nestle's bars, Alfred."

Alf leaned on his hand against the breakfast bar it had taken him and George the best part of a month to build:

"Give us a mo, I'm enjoying watching that daft lot."

He wondered if an old woman dancing with her daughter and granddaughter, sliding around in slippers and turban, was what the song-writers intended? But, when you boiled it down, wasn't that what life was all about?

Never too old

Too past it

Not the oldest swinger in town

And what would it matter if you bleddy were?

They were savouring the music, as they had with the Andrews Sisters during wartime. "Not the bleddy boogie-woogie-bugle-boy again," Alf used to laugh. Someone like Win rejoicing 'till they died, no matter what fate threw at them. They'd lost family, and friends in both wars, lost Beryl's Mam and Shirl's sister, Rita, at a young age, yet here they were, jumping up and down and laughing like cats.

Alf roused himself, and went to find those chocolate bars (George hoarded chocolate, now it was readily available, as if there was going to be another conflict. "You'll spend up" said Old Man Cole at the Grocer's, "you and them Nestle's."

"I'm not going to be richest bogger in the graveyard.'" George had responded. "Where would that get us? Remember the war, that old bird who took bags of money down the Anderson?"

"Mrs Swales?"

"Ah."

"She died just as war finished, and all that brass had done her no good. Scrimping all her life – it bought her a lovely stone, did that, and the rest went to relatives in Surrey

17

she'd never heard on. She hadn't written owt down to say who got it."

"Mebbe you're right, George."

"I know I bleddy am."

Alf and George wolfed their bars with satisfaction.

"Come on Alf," Beryl called, "stop gorging and give it a go."

"Why not?"

So Alf joined the dance, newly lit fag dangling perilously over the rug.

Years later, when he watched a television re-run of the Miss Marple film *Murder at the Gallop*, Alf had seen Margaret Rutherford and Stringer Davis get up to dance the twist – Her with mop of snowy curls and black-net frock, him with slicked white hair and a resigned expression. Alf had laughed, with a rising lump in his throat, thinking how, if an old girl with a determined expression was on the floor, sooner or later, you'd join her. "This is Mr Stringer's favourite dance," Rutherford told the Inspector, who looked-on, bemused.

Alf had thought of Win, George, a sunburst mirror he'd paid double its worth in the winning of. "Twist and bleddy shout, Win," he'd whispered. Because life, for all folk knew, could end this second, this breath, and such dancing eked-out every dreg.

Grandwem and George, Shirl and Beryl, George Formby... That living room which seemed like it would be there forever... Alf had looked at the screen to watch Rutherford and Davis twist gamely on, somewhere hearing laughter, shoes scraping, the click, click, click of budgie seed hitting a patent-white handbag.

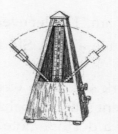

Miss Almandine Soap

It was all in the open and known bar the shouting. Beryl had blurted it out to Grandwem – pregnancy news shared as they left the *Co-Op*. "Thank the Lord for that," Grandwem thought. Luckily, the confession hadn't been overheard by any of the town's tattle-tales. Grandwem had turned to witness Beryl's streaming eyes and shaking lower-lip, and thought she looked as she did when David Coverley had snatched and eaten her biscuit at the school gate. She couldn't find it in her heart to be mad at her granddaughter.

"I know, Love." She said.

"How do you know? I'm not that fat am I?"

"You're my little lass, 'course I bleddy knew. Besides, you've always fair hated liquorice, and you've shoved 'bootlaces' down yer neck for a month or more."

"Does George know?"

"No. No bogger does. I've said nowt. Thought it were best. But I'll have to tell George, now. Maybe I'll tell the budgie first, and he'll let him know. Whatever, we'll all sit down and decide what's to be done."

"Grandwem?"

"What?"

"I've made a mess, and I'm so sorry, but I don't want it."

"Why?"

"I want to stay as I am. I've let everybody down."

"Hush, we'll all have a chat, Shirl and Alf, too. In the meantime, say nowt."

Beryl went off work sick for a week or two, Grandwem writing to management on her behalf, quoting glandular fever, and promise of a doctor's note to follow. Soon after, one Sunday, after lunch, Grandwem treated Shirl, Beryl, and Alf to a round at the pub, determining to tell George over a brown ale at home. Resolved not to let things fester, she opened and poured two ales, then told George everything at a go, laying down facts as they stood, and not ornamenting a word. She finished with: "So that's it, like it or lump it, as dogs do dumplings."

George's face drained to the same colour as the oatmeal-tinted antimacassar on his chair-back.

"Does she want it?"

"No, but she's having it."

"Bleddy hell. I didn't think our Beryl was the sort."

"Well, she's not, but that doesn't alter the fact. As far as I can see she's made one mistake."

"Yeah, but it were a reet belter."

They sat, supping foam from brown ale.

"Win, it'll ruin her if she has it."

"It'll ruin her if she don't. If you're considering Ida Medway, George, forget it. She's killed as many lasses as cured. They say there's unmentionables under her yard."

George thought of tiny Mrs Medway with her grey pinnie and face like cut wood. She hadn't occurred to him as a solution. "I'd never let Ida Medway near our Beryl," he sniffed, "you should know that. But some girls, though,

20

they get desperate if they don't want them and they're cornered. You know it, Win."

"I do, but I didn't know you did."

"I warn't turfed-up under a cabbage, or born yesterday, if that's what you think. Some blokes follow balloons for hoss-muck, but I'm not one of them. Win, do you recall Cora Rains?"

"Aye, poor lass."

"Well, she were my cousin."

"I'd forgotten, besides, it wouldn't be like that, now, George."

"Wouldn't it?"

"Things 's moved on."

Grandwem didn't sound that convinced as she said it. "Have they, Win? Do you really think they have? Here? I keep reading all this permissive this and that in the paper, but those old lasses who're quick to condemn aren't part of it all. Do you think Mansfield's changed that much, Win, 'cos I bleddy don't."

Win thought back to Cora Rains, feeling her blood turn to ice cream. Cora had been the prettiest girl in the hosiery factory, and one of the cleverest. She'd replaced Ellie Booth as forewoman, after fiery Ellie had told the manager to "Stick his job up his fat arse." Cora was half Ellie's age, and was head of a group of workers at just twenty-three. Soon, a smart new coat and hat attested to Cora's wage rise. Close her eyes, and Grandwem could picture auburn curls poking from beneath the grey regulation cap, slim ankles delicate beneath a shapeless shift. Cora had hazel eyes framed by a double layer of lashes that would've been the envy of a film star.

There'd been that bother, the year of Cora's undoing, over a national search for a girl to be the face of Almandine Soap, the soap that "washed skin lovelier." A few months before that, it'd been Miss Lux, a contest Grandwem herself had been in the running for. But Miss Lux had been nowhere near as big a search as Miss Almandine. Miss Almandine was a brand with fat money behind it, and no mistake. It was said photographers were scouring the country searching for the right girl, and there were tales of film contracts that must follow such a prestigious win.

Even if those contracts were just a rumour, the winner would be featured on posters, calendars, and magazine advertisements, then toured around the country. One of their kind could become that story issuing hope to others, of the girl plucked from nowhere to become a star – and it had happened to some – like Agnes de Lynne, "The Kinematograph Girl", who'd been discovered working in a shop. Just think, a factory worker, shop hand, or mill girl, her face gracing a thousand billboards.

No one but Cora had met Mr Trail, the man claiming to be the Almandine Soap official photographer. Cora got talking to him at the bar of the Bell Inn in Nottingham, after arriving there with a friend who'd soon copped off with a lonely soldier. Staying in The Bell, alone, would have condemned the girl in the eyes of some. But she could still see her friend, and wanted to make sure the soldier wouldn't try anything too fresh.

Mr Trail had introduced himself by flashing a gilt-edged card and telling Cora she was by far the best of all the girls he'd seen. He implied in the strongest terms his search might be over. He'd persuaded her back to the studio he'd rented for the company while staying in Nottingham. All this relayed in hushed tones by Cora's erstwhile friend, Pop March, who claimed the bit about the soldier was lies.

"And, I heard, he got her to that 'studio' and it weren't so much of a photographer's workplace as a bedroom wi' a pot plant and a curtain. She told me he did take some pictures, but then, well, he took advantage. She were afraid to say owt, or maybe she liked him more than she's letting on. And she tried to make *me* look like a strumpet!"

A few months down the line, and Cora who seemed to be putting on a bit of weight, vomited over a machine at work. She'd been taken for a medical appointment and sacked on the spot a week later. There were no references, Pop whispered.

"Mam said friends and family all shut doors on her as soon as it were known," said George, as if reading Grandwem's thoughts. "My Mam allus regretted it, but her Mam, and others told kith and kin to show no mercy. Pop told everyone Cora'd tried all sorts of potions, but nowt worked. She came to us all for help, and the whole town just about turned its back. In the end, she had it alone, in the workhouse, and they took it off her. Three weeks after, they came and told her it were dead."

George gulped. "My Mam said cold-shouldering Cora were the worst mistake she made in her life. She said it made us all worse people, all but... Hey, do you know, I said the whole town turned its back, but I were lying to you. That manager at the Factory, the one Ellie Booth told to shove his job up his fat arse, paid her way out of the workhouse, and he and his wife paid for Cora's digs. And no one spoke to them for months, either."

Grandwem's lips pursed. "I only recall Cora slightly after she came out,' she mused. 'Din't she become one of them women as knocks on folk's doors?"

"Ah. She'd knock, you'd think she wanted money, but she just used to stand there. Then she'd say 'I'm looking for my little boy, I heard a baby crying within and thought it was him. I'm sorry for wasting your time.' Then she'd go. Poor Cora, white as milk she were."

"I've forgot what happened to her, George."

"They found her dead, in Mester Bainbridge's outhouse, that year it snowed. Family hadn't been outside, only to t'lavvy, and he had that old building that used to be a stable for his dad's hosses. Said she was just lying on a pile of old coats and blankets, looking-up at a hole in the roof. Her coat was swaddled in her arms, and it looked for all the world as if she were holding a babby."

"Exposure?"

"Ah. It were always a mystery to me, Win, why she wanted that child after how it were conceived."

"Mebbe she thought summat good came from all that rubbish, we'll not know, now."

Grandwem sucked at what was left of her pint, then went and poured herself and George another. "It's no good." She said. "I apologise to you, George, about Ida Medway, I know Beryl's your little lass, too. But you're right about the town, change or no, it's still full of righteous boggers that'll make mince-meat of her. No, she'll have to go away, and have it. Then we'll see what can be done."

George leant forward, taking his wife's hand. "You're a good woman, Win Bean, but we're much too old to take-on a kiddie, if that's what you were thinking."

"I wasn't, I know we're old as Methuselah, but we'll have to sort something. No Great Grandchild of mine's being given away like a free ring in a cereal box."

George looked at Win's determined face and shuddered into his pint.

"Hey," she said, "I've just remembered a bit of Cora's story I'd forgotten."

"What's that?"

"You'll remember when I say it, Love. A few weeks after Cora got sacked, the real Almandine Soap man turned-up at the factory, looking for girls. Anyway, Pop quizzed him while he were there, said he'd never heard of Mr Trail, and that he was the company's only East Midland's Representative. Not that knowing this made Pop any sweeter towards Cora. In the end, though, "Mr Almandine Soap" did choose a girl from round here to go through, Elsie Brown, but her Dad, like mine with the Lux people, wouldn't let her do it. Said having your daughter's face on a poster for the whole town to see was vulgar, and no girl of his was going to bring disgrace on the family by doing that.

Fairy Tale

"Once upon a bleddy time,' 'cos that's a Nottingham version of how good fairy tales begin... "

Hang about, though, maybe this isn't one of those good stories, so who knows if it will have that "they lived happily ever after" tagged-onto its end?

Any road, once upon a bleddy time, there was a street.

It wasn't a posh street full of mucky swanks, them people as'll charge you tuppence to sit on their sofas, and it wasn't a particularly good looking street, either. The houses were all back-to-backs, and they had outside lavvies, which some might take as proof of low status, or even no status, truth be told. "Outside lavvies are all right, they're where men go to whistle, read the paper, and avoid family strife," Grandwem Win, our tale's fairy godmother, might claim.

Any road up, it was one of them streets where most knew each other's business, and many households were related (though not in a webbed-finger way, Win would hasten to add, oh, and nor did people leave toes in their socks).

Well, on this ordinary street, in a fairly-ordinary town, which had (more-or-less) come through a war unscathed, lived a couple. The couple (who came through the same war pretty much unscathed, though now missing her sister and a brother-in-law) were married. They'd hitched fairly-late in life, during wartime, and had been busy in the years ever since.

The man worked, like many of his kind, at this and that, and favoured many coloured kipper ties, greyhounds with decorative names, and a pencil thin moustache. The woman also worked hard though, it might be said, more legitimately.

Anyway, the couple were so busy it never occurred to them, until too late, they were missing something – and what they were missing was small and stork brought. By the time they realised this, there seemed little they could do.

"We've been fools,' said the woman, 'and now we're too old."

"Do you reckon?' Said the man, folding his *Sporting Chance*."

"We're old, not as old as some, but we are and that's a fact. Just think, we could have given a kiddie a better home than many."

The man didn't mind so much, he had the dogs, his pub visits, and the rest, but he hated to see his wife glum. She took to brooding in her spare hours and looked (he said) "more miserable than death's missus."

Would it have been a blue basinet or pink for their spare room? How would a combination of her winning-personality and his guile have turned-out?

Of course, it wasn't that the woman hadn't got anyone to love. There was her hubby, and Grandwem Win, George, and Little Beryl, daughter of her long dead sister. Plus, there was their Billy, then Grandwem's last brother, Uncle Norrie and his pups, not to mention those dogs they all cherished. Even the budgie was lovable.

Yet still…

As with all good tales, time passed, things went on, mewling pups were born onto blankets on the floor of old Norrie's gypsy caravan near Blaby Copse, and rubbed into life by the cast-iron stove… smoke rising through it and up a pipe under his chimney, as if a new Pope were being announced. And then something happened to jolt the whole family, as it turned out Little Beryl wasn't quite so little after all.

For weeks, no one voiced anything, just viewed Beryl's expanding frock in the stomach area with alarm. Except, one tea time at Norrie's, the woman's husband said: "Ayup Beryl, you'll soon wax as fat as me." And she burst into tears, seeking a nearby field, beyond Norrie's caravan and the copse, and sobbing into one of the pups as if it was a fur hankie. After that there'd been silences, recriminations, whispers, and finally a confession big as a house – told by Grandwem Win in the style of the radio's *Man in Black*.

"And the thing is," Grandwem concluded, "she knows she's been a daft beggar, but she's not getting rid, so don't waste your breath suggesting it. Long and short of it is, she'll have her baby, and go away to do it, but after, she don't want it. We'll have to find folk as'll tek it."

"She don't want it?" Said the woman, "well! I love our Beryl to death, but I call that wicked. There's plenty would love the chance."

"I know, Love, but she's not one of them. These young people with interesting jobs want something else, summat a washing line of nappies can't provide. It's not as you or I would think, but there it is. Imagine growing up with yer Mam resenting you and thinking she could have had a big career in costume. No, it's there, like it or not."

29

"So, what's happening, Win?" said the man: "give it to us."

"She's going away now its showing, to Mrs Campsie's boarding house in Blackpool, and then, soon as it's born and she's ready, it'll go to be adopted. I'm going with her, and will sort things out with the adoption people. Work think she's going away to recover from a bad bout of a glandular illness. They say she can come back when she's ready."

"But it's your Great Grandchild! It would have been Rita and Kenny's first Grandkid!"

"It can't be helped, love. Beryl says with no fella she'll be shunned, and it'll be shunned, and I reckon she's right."

"But to give it away, right away, like it was an unwanted parcel! When some people'd give their eye-teeth!"

And the woman wept like a child, and her husband saw, for the first time, what she was reaching at, and gulped. He went outside, lit a fag, smoked it, and returned. He'd thought about long dead Rita, long dead Kenny, and what lovely Grandparents they'd have made.

"I think what my wife's trying to say, Win," he said to those assembled, "is that if Beryl wanted the nipper to stay in the family, we'd be happy to oblige. We couldn't afford owt when Rita died, so we couldn't bring Beryl up, but things's a bit brighter now. I know we're not love's young wotsit, but we've still lots to give before that man in black comes knockin'."

"Oh, Alfred!" said Grandwem, "You solid gold boy!"

More talk. And, as in good, realistic fairy tales, meant for a grown-up audience as much as for the kiddies, more arguing. After these, things were sort of resolved.

The woman and Grandwem would go and live alongside Beryl in Blackpool until the baby was due. They'd say she was in a convalescent place, poorly, to folk at home, and put her weight-gain down to her illness, plus "a medication".

"They thought it were glandular fever," George would say, "but it were summat to do with glands as meks you fat." As he would remark later, lots of folk would own up to having had the same condition.

Meanwhile, the man would spread it around that he and his wife had been secretly looking to adopt a child, and that one had been found for them in Manchester. The man said his wife had been away with Beryl, and that he was going to Manchester to meet her and sign the relevant papers. "What a rigmarole," he said to George, "I haven't lied this much since I were at school."

So, as in all good fairy tales, the characters got various happy endings. The man and his wife (who were, as was hinted hugely, called Shirley and Alfred) came home with a lovely baby girl, Little Rita, who they said was a late gift meant only for them. Grandwem and George got to keep their Great-grandchild. And Beryl, who was Little Beryl no more, went back to the job she loved, having sworn Mrs Campsie to silence. All as if someone had waved a wand.

But...

As with most of these tales there were complications, especially as in those involving babies, fairy godmothers, and convenient fibbing.

For gifts, as every reader knows, arrive with both blessings and curses.

For every Princess Aurora, there's a poisoned spindle.

For each Snow White, an apple.

For every pig, a ham sandwich ...

And for every Beryl, a condition.

She had her kiddie. Gave it to her Auntie and Uncle, who from here-on-in in the story became the child's Mum and Dad. These loved the girl more than anything, and would give her all they had and more besides... but from the moment that our story's couple took the child, the baby was theirs, and Beryl was a bystander. She even had a new name, "Auntie Beryl", for the baby to learn.

As if someone had shaken a magic wand, "Mum" became "Auntie Beryl" for all time. So, our couple lived in their ordinary street, in that almost ordinary town, with their extraordinary late child. And, if the woman ever noticed a hint of longing in Auntie Beryl's voice she had to hold the child close and whisper, "Look at your Auntie, doesn't she look lovely?" Before turning away. And, despite the magic wand, the woman had to believe they'd all live happily ever after.

Thus, Shirl wrote in her pink diary with its blue clasp, the one Beryl had bought her for Christmas. This was the story she'd give Little Rita one day, as a coming-of-age gift. She was sure she would. This was the first story she'd ever write down for her daughter, but not, if she'd only have known it, the last.

PLACES WE BELONG

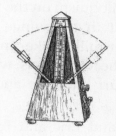

Wishee

It gave Court a real kick to see how much Billy relished the phrase on their top billing: "COOPER AND BEAN - AS SEEN ON YOUR SCREEN."

Not that their TV show didn't matter to Court, it was solid gold at a time when most older acts were settling for electro-plate. That air-force-blue poster also bore the legend "YOUR FAVOURITE DUO AS WISHEE AND WASHEE - DOUBLE TROUBLE FOR ALADDIN."

But who were those others gracing the bill? Some singing sensation teenage girls went mad for, also off the box, three lads looking like Ringo, George and Paul without the sarky one, and Barry Davina, a TV ventriloquist whose fondness for the ales was matched only by his long-standing affair with the bookies.

Course, Court and Billy knew all the names of the fillers not making it on to the poster: "Nandorino and his Dogs of Wonder", "Billy May, the Lady Divine" among them, acts who'd grafted for ENSA and sung at countless Stage Door Canteens and factories up and down the country when nation called. Acts who could be relied upon to do the business. "Nandorino and his pooches may be old-hat, but that poodle's a better ventriloquist than bloody Barry

Davina, at least you don't see its lips move. I blame bleeding Archie Andrews, ventriloquism on the radio, Bill, I ask you!" It stung Court to wait in the wings seeing Davina's lips move like a Manchester mill worker miming over the din of their machine. No, the older acts were suffering from a surfeit of the box. Court knew he and Bill were the lucky ones.

Apart from them, and Eric and Ernie, most headliners these days were too slickly televisual for Court: compères who smarmed over ordinary people grateful for winning a few shillings, singers with too many teeth... What about that spark of talent that couldn't be learned in studio? What about that thing you couldn't imitate that made audiences gasp, night after night? Court thought of Vi, the woman he'd loved and lost ages back. Sometimes he thought he'd see her turn up at a studio somewhere, but old hands like her hardly seemed to arrive these days.

There was Court's protégé, Ernie Fields, who'd become a big stage star but couldn't seem to do right on TV. Ernie was a lovely song and dance man, who seemed to have starlight in his stage-shoes. But Ernie's wit and natural flair for a number didn't seem to translate well enough to the small screen.

"I don't get it," Billy said one night, after Ernie had guested on THE BOYS MOST LIKELY TO, COOPER AND BEAN AT THE BBC, "he knocks spots off most singers with their own shows. Yet we guest him, Morecambe and Wise have had him on more than once at ATV, but he never steps further than the front gate. Maybe his name's too close to Ernie Wise."

But Court knew what Ernie hadn't got going for him.

Something about Ernie Fields's under-nourishment as a kid playing Karniko's appalling Variety Tent, under fed and out in all weathers, had stuck with him. On stage it was glued back with greasepaint and whitened out by many lights. But on screen the lights were different, harsher somehow, and despite Ernie's winning grin and bright eyes his head looked a little too large for his body on the box, his hands a bit too big, flopping about from scraggy wrists. Evening suits only emphasised that lean frame, and made you wonder why there wasn't a bigger man inside. Glove hands and something of cabbage soup in his complexion did for him, Court thought.

Despite early promise and chances, Ernie wasn't going to make the TV big-time. That Cooper and Bean, longer in the teeth than most and with a clear look of demob about them had done so, still filled Court with awe.

Even parts in panto and such were changing now. Wishee Washee was a single turn, always had been, but now, to accommodate "THE BOYS MOST LIKELY TO", it was showing as a double-act. "Think of all those great Window Twankeys and others," Court said as they got ready one morning, "Dan Leno, George Robey, Little Tich, learning their stagecraft over years and refining and refining. Tich did for himself physically, Leno lost his mind, and Robey kept performing until they had to carry him on in a chair... Yet to be in panto now, you've just got to be seen on the telly, and I include us in that."

"Yes, and I'll add to it, Courtney; some of the acts we looked-up to and were great, really great, well there's nothing of them."

"Sid Field." Court rejoined.

37

"Sid Field, exactly. Those big films he made weren't representative of the act, and he bloody knew it. And *Harvey*, genius on stage, but Jimmy Stewart in the movie, Hollywood."

"Hollywood. Sid Field died during a run of *Harvey*, I think I'm right saying that. All that graft, six or so years at the top, then dead. Films that didn't do him justice, a few radio interviews, I mean, people like us listened to every breath he took. Poor Sid, I fear he was the best of us. Long gone, now…"

"Ollie," Billy was doing his best Stan Laurel, "was he our exhausted leader?"

"He certainly was, Stanley." Court did an Oliver Hardy bashful gesture with his tie, managing to be both galumphing and elegant.

"Funny, ain't it? Sid missing all this TV malarkey."

"Wonder if he'd've taken to it?"

"We'll never know."

Court and Billy's "Wishee Washee" robes were parakeet green, pink-edged as glossed lollipops. Mandarin caps boasted oversized gilt tassels, and blue sateen slippers bore wire toes, turned up at ridiculously large angles. To dance in these, they had to be acrobatic as Little Tich, famous for balancing on outsized shoes. A lesser act would've come to grief and, Court was sure, landed arse-up in the orchestra pit.

Despite initially desiring Fu Manchu moustaches, they'd been informed by management (which now included TV studio representatives) that they had to keep their faces bare to look like their on-screen personas. This had become regarded as imperative since a child seeing ATV star Harry Mugglestone, from *Mugglestone's Gap*, where he played an irascible pub-landlord, had cried itself sick because he was unrecognisable under the big beard he wore as Long John Silver in *Treasure Island*.

"*Treasure Island*'s not a bleedin' panto anyway," Court had remonstrated.

"It is now, old son, and that kid nearly did itself a mischief bawlin' 'it's not him, Mam, I want us money back.'"

"We're Wishee and Washee,

we've come to do your laundry,

straight from your TV,

we're Wishee and Washee

our washing's never squashy,

yes, Wishee and Washee are we."

They'd dance across the stage, holding a long purple silk robe between them. At one point, they'd twist the robe and it became a string of flags of many lands. Sometimes, they varied the effect so doves flew from it.

In the theatre lobby were programmes for sale, miniature plastic television sets in red, with stickers of Billy and Court's faces inside them, and tacky yellow plastic lamps reading COOPER AND BEAN - FROM YOUR TV SCREEN. The lamps didn't light, but kids seemed to go for them. Billy always saved a bit of whatever merchandise there was for Grandwem, who was accumulating quite a selection of programmes, and objects that sat on a specially erected Formica shelf above the telly.

"Who'd a thought it, our Billy and Courtney on a plastic telly, lovely." she said, Billy knowing that she ordered souvenirs from each show for most of her neighbours.

"Just think, Sunnyside Terrace awash with our ugly mugs,' laughed Court."

39

"We're Wishee and Washee,

our songs are rarely naughty,

not so your kids'd see,

yes, Wishee and Washee,

you can clock us nightly,

on Wishee and Washee TV."

Court realised they should be grateful. Mad Dan Leno, the greatest of the Victorian halls, dying tortured by his demons, difficult to work with, where once he'd been a joy... Yes, he and Bill were lucky, happy and top of the bill, top of the polls.

Recognised. Fêted.

Yet, he missed the old shows where he'd known both acts and hands, missed nights ending with a backstage brown ale. Now, they were often whisked off to corporate events in the bigger, American-owned hotels, a car coming for them.

He recalled his first panto. *Cinderella*, years before he'd teamed up with Billy. He'd been a chorus boy, given his own spot when it was found he could caper like a resurrected Dan Leno. He'd been a kid then, grafting, same as Ernie Fields in Karniko's tent. Before he met Grandwem, Beryl, Shirl and Alf, and become part of Billy's family. How he could have done with a tenacious old bird like Grandwem advising him in those early days! Funny, but try as he might, and even looking at an old photograph (where the young Win looked surprisingly like her older self) he couldn't really imagine her without turban, pinnie, wrinkles...

Closing his eyes, Court could still see his young self in the spot for his brief caper. Feel that rising eagerness to please, that terror of no re-bookings and the rent to pay for digs, the fear of it all being done before it was really started...

The kid was slender, white suit once belonging to another act, a little too large around the gills, but his wide smile made-up for it. He'd had that lucky trick of making an audience like him. On stage, Ernie Fields had that, too, but not, like Court, on the box. No, Court and Billy were lucky all right:

"I'm Wishee... he's Washee..."

Somewhere, Court sensed a grin from that boy he'd been. Feet making light of a soft-shoe-shuffle:

"Our show is rather showy,

you can see we do it nightly,

yes, Wishee and Washee are we."

"Here's to you, lad," he thought, and took a bow.

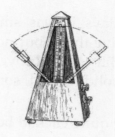

Washee

Cooper and Bean were gold as the egg laid by the panto goose, Billy thought.

Heading the bill, cheered by ebullient crowds at evening performances, matinees, specials, and on the box. On the wall of their dressing room he now hung a print of one of his favourite pictures, a crowded balcony at the old Bedford music hall, by Walter Sickert. At least, someone told him it was the Bedford. Billy had bought the print from a box of rolled-up papers outside a Charing Cross bookseller's years ago. He'd framed it and it had become his lucky picture. But the lettering, saying what it was of, had obviously been on a little raised tag, half gone before he had it. All the tag now said was *Hall – Sickert*. But that crowd, yelling, whooping, their faces yellow and ecstatic in the gaslight, Billy thought of them as his people from the off.

Court and he had their real people, too, their cheers were all they'd grafted for, and they were comics in clover.

Since Ruby, Billy's erstwhile flame, returned from America (brought back by Grandwem and George after a miss-aimed fling with Mr Redbush the third) she was in clover too. Not always with him, though – even if in public she was often his girl, accompanying him to premieres and events. She was singing again, her voice lovely as ever, but she'd missed her bigger chances on the London scene, and

43

she knew it. Nowadays it was smart supper-clubs and boats, she'd always have them, but not the elite venues she should have filled. Billy and Ruby had separate London apartments, separate holidays and, sometimes, separate love affairs.

While things never quite clicked between him and Ruby, they'd not gone away. "Young people don't want wedding bells, I realise." Grandwem had said, "I thought we had a war so you lot could settle down but that were a daft idea. So long as you're happy, though."

"I'm not that young, Ma."

"Well, you are to me. I'm ewd as sin's Grandma, I know, but you're my lad. You are happy aren't you?"

"You know me. I did think when she came back and left Mr Redbush for good, we'd get spliced. But I got the TV, and she got those club and ocean liner dates, and somehow it never quite materialised."

He recalled when he'd said that, Grandwem (who'd been doing the pots with him at the time) sucked her teeth and scraped at a dish so viciously Billy thought it a wonder the Indian Tree pattern hadn't come off.

And, complications with Ruby aside, everything was hunky-dory. Faces on posters, glossy programmes, miniature plastic televisions. "Ere, Mam, that's them," an excited child had gasped, as he and Court entered the theatre. "Ere, they're dead famous, look. On the box and everythink."

Daily, they autographed pictures of themselves, smiled and waved, Savile-Row-cut coats immaculate under artificial light. Those books they signed, with their black leather covers, and fondant pink and green tracing-paper in thin sheets within, reminded Billy of Court's new obsession, old signed cards.

Like Beryl's love of aged postcards, passed on from Grandwem Win's big album, Court was coveting those decorated with acts from the past. His apartment, and their shared dressing-rooms were bearing the brunt. Shoe boxes full of them, under chairs, below stools, loose cards filling drawers. Some in albums tied with fading ribbon, other cards stacked: hand tinted; spangled; sketched; sepia; black and white; on card; paper; silk; greens pinks and lilacs like the Ladurée macaroons Ruby craved.

Whenever she, Beryl, or Grandwem visited, Court couldn't keep their hands off chorus girls from long gone revues, clutching dogs or dolls, hats so large they seemed giant lilies. "Oh, aren't they lovely? So innocent. Just think some poor boy probably took one to the front with him." Ruby gasped.

She had a point. The cards made Billy think of Mattie, Grandwem's brother, a boy sporting a man's coat, squinting for the camera before being marched off to die in the shout before last. And the cards that soldiers had bought were now cheap and discarded, like their messages of hope and love. Court didn't often buy himself big things, Billy thought, they were still on the road too much for that, despite fancy addresses. The cards were portable, just, and brought him a lot of pleasure.

Billy smiled as he recalled "Alfie's Repeater" the large clock Court purchased during the war. They'd been in Bournemouth and Court had seen it in an antique shop at the Westcliffe Arcade, swearing it had been in his family, and naming it after some relative or other. Billy couldn't quite recall the ins-and-outs, but Grandwem had it still, a brown monster of a clock, that had chimed the length of Bournemouth's streets as they'd carried it back to digs. No, the cards were a safer bet.

Of course, it wasn't just the soldier's favourites Court collected, now, it seemed that, as well as cards of all the greats, Vesta Tilley, George Formby senior, and the Mighty Rosco among them, he was collecting cards of panto characters, and as many from *Aladdin* as he could find. He loved the old "oriental" magic acts, too, their gowns and silk caps a version of he and Billy's current costumes.

They were all Wishee and Washee, pulling faces and about as truly 'oriental' as Grandwem Win. Skipping, hopping, gurning, is that how he and Court would appear frozen for future generations? "Mekkin monkeys of yus sens," as George had it.

Billy imagined a future family watching them on a giant screen, unable to make head-nor-tail of it. He imagined someone with shoe-boxes full of pictures, albums, plastic televisions, the faces of two half-recalled characters grinning out.

"We're temporary," he whispered. And thought, for all their striving and graft, he was right. Daft to consider otherwise, Dan Leno was recorded as the first Twankey, named after some long forgotten tea, but Mark Sheridan? Who recalled his capering and "here we are again" quadrille now?

In a dark wooden box on their dressing-table at the BBC, Billy had Court's birthday present, a small square form resembling a *Strand* packet and already wrapped in white tissue tied with blue ribbon. Billy anticipated his friend's opening it in front of cast and crew, or maybe in a moment just shared by the two of them, him relishing the awe and wonder on Court's face.

A little junk shop in an alley off Fleet Street (quite close to Ye Olde Cheshire Cheese, the jet-black Dickensian looking pub where Billy had enjoyed a solo lunch one day) had provided it. He'd sauntered from The Cheese deciding to wander to walk-off the heavy gammon steak he'd treated himself to.

The shop's window had been filthy, and amused him with a battered selection of oddments for sale, including a single pepper-pot in the shape of a sailor boy, broken nutcrackers formed as legs, and the worst example of a stuffed squirrel known to humanity.

Billy had laughed so hard at the furry gargoyle in squirrel form, he'd leaned in to get a better look. There he noticed a small framed picture to the creature's right, that caught his breath. A square card no bigger than your palm, encased in glass with a paper frame stuck on, hand decoration meant to resemble wood.

But it was who was within that frame which had made Billy gasp and blink. George Robey, "the Prime Minister of Mirth".

Dead nearly a decade. Billy had been at his funeral, as had Court. A maestro he'd been, violin maker, athlete, artist and musician. Billy recalled the huge dark eyebrows framing his potato face, his comic walk, and cheerful smile. Since the funeral, he'd scarcely brought him to mind. Robey had come to specialise in farewell tours, each outing seeing him frailer, like one of those white-topped seeds blown from a dandelion.

The last performance Billy and Court attended had seen the old stager carried on in a chair. It was just before Robey

47

died, and the lump in Billy's throat made him feel as though in some way the Prime Minister was already gone. The act had been delivered like King Lear dividing his lands, the audience had stood and cheered until words were drowned.

Taking curtain calls from the chair, he'd stretched veiny hands wide, grinning at those yelling, affectionate blobs from Billy's lucky picture. And what about the picture in the junk shop window? Did that, likewise, do Robey justice? Well, it should have done, as the performer created the image himself.

The man depicted in a few inky lines was all stage-business, composed of grin, chubby face, and charcoal brows - his raspberry nose was eight strokes wide, lips rolled themselves around a silent phrase, eyes twinkled. It had become legend how if "Mirth's PM" had time and inclination, he'd sign his autograph by sketching an ink self-portrait. Billy had never seen one until the junk shop window, and its magnificent honesty pulled him up short. He giggled, remembering one of the many catch-phrases: "I haven't come here to be laughed at." He'd gone in and purchased it for Court on the spot. Once it was wrapped, he'd written his own autograph on a slim card which he'd attached to the gift:

"To Wishee,

from Washee.

Many Happy Returns of the Day

from the Prime Minister's Seat."

48

Her Boy Ted

Ivy West wasn't one for swearing. But today she was thinking of every rotten word she'd heard uttered in the lounge downstairs, and more bloody besides. "Arse," she muttered to the reflection in her dressing-table's mirror, "No, arses."

Her punters would be shocked.

She knew she appeared increasingly ladylike and old-fashioned to them. Hell-fire lips, rouged cheeks in the same *Bourgeois* dusky pink shade she'd been using from similar paper pots for years, and not a stray hair escaping from the style she'd pin-curled since the war. Pin-curls, when fresh girls were sporting beehives, that dated her. Girl no more, sauntering from dressing-table to bed, from bed to window.

A stray white feather was spiralling on chilly air. Maybe a gull's. "I 'ate gulls, they're rats wiv beaks," Ted, her black sheep of a son had said. "Vermin. There's a lot of vermin in this town, Ma. Make no mistake!"

And… hadn't he known them all?

The spivs, chancers, ne'er-do-wells his school friends managed to steer-clear of. Look where it had got him - any nice school pals vanishing like melted cornets when they (or their parents) clocked Ted's associates.

49

Ivy laughed a bleak "Ha" into the stale bedroom. She opened the window. That feather, which had landed on the sill, was borne up again. "Rats wiv beaks." Ted had been able to spot a rat all right.

There were holidaying couples with children on the street below, kids dutifully holding-hands with parents and clutching buckets and spades in free fingers. They'd get a shock on Brighton's pebbles, Ivy thought. Older pairs with young adults joining in conversation also caught her eye, nice smart boys in grey trousers with olive green sweaters. Boys who'd be doing apprenticeships or courses at technical colleges. Unlike her boy, unable for the moment to walk freely down the street. Not that Ted *was* a boy anymore. Despite his small stature, he was a young man, and growing older by the hour.

Ivy recalled all those American films highlighting *Trouble with Today's Twisted Youth*. Those films had been popular since the fifties, and showed no sign of petering out. *Out for Kicks and to Hell with Tomorrow* read the strap-lines, they didn't know the half of it.

'Ten minutes to opening time,' Ivy whispered to the feather's new resting spot on the window's top. Ten minutes and she'd be all smiles. Greeting her first customer, Old Toff, who practically lived in the mild-brown booth near the front window: "Thought you were going to open late today, Gel," he'd say as usual, before settling for a pint and a sleep. She'd smile and smile through smoke and chatter, joining in without listening, wondering how many of her regulars knew she had a grown son inside.

Then there was Lesley Jones, the new girl, who said she'd done bar-work before, but had she heck as like. Ivy'd never seen so much spilled ale, miscounted change, bags of crisps given to the wrong people. It's like *Take Your Pick* in here, Toff chortled one afternoon. Lesley was pretty, with her short ash-blonde hair tied in a blue chiffon scarf, candy-floss lips, and rows of lashes. Ivy knew some lads frequented The Cricketers' because they fancied their chances. Not that Lesley appeared remotely interested. So long as she didn't show any interest in Ted when he got out, nobody needed that brand of aggravation in their lives, Ivy thought.

It was Lesley who'd got everything ready this morning, going out for a wander and leaving the door unlocked in her wake. Ivy should be down there, really, but the closed sign was still in the window, and the regulars weren't ones for turning-up before time. Someone could come and help himself to a swift half, but it had never happened before.

Ivy reached up high, disturbing air around the settled feather. It floated down and she caught it between thumb and forefinger. Downy edges reminded her of those bigger feathers sewn to costumes, tickling away at your shoulders, itching thighs as you did your best to look glamourous. She'd been a looker once, and now think of it, pulling pints for years and no opportunity to go back on the halls. Still, she thought of all those closing halls, now hosting nudie shows or bingo nights, once fresh gilding peeling like an old girl's makeup.

Her reverie was broken by sounds of the door opening to the bar downstairs. She knew she ought to have been there earlier.

"Just my luck, Burglar Bill," she whispered, letting the feather fall. She'd go down and confront him, take a brass candlestick in case he needed clonking. Then she heard the familiar call.

"Ma, are you about?"

Her Ted.

"Ma. Ma. It's me."

But he wasn't due out for a week. She'd had the official letter and everything. It wasn't until the twenty-sixth. Christ on a bike! It *was* the twenty-sixth. The dresser's gilt calendar said it, plain as day. She'd been working a good week behind.

"Ted?"

"Yeah. I knew you wouldn't send no brass band, but I fought you might meet me off the bus from Lewes."

"Oh, Ted, love, I'm sorry, sorry. I'm looking at the calendar now - I was a week off."

She'd made it to the stairs' top as he approached their base, waiting for her to come down.

"Ma,' he shouted, 'can I help myself to a wet? I'm parched."

She called "Yes", making her way downstairs to him.

The man standing behind the bar didn't look like her Ted at all. It was as though his younger edges had been knapped away, leaving something hard as cut-flint in their place. A scar's red thread ran from the side of one eye to the top of his cheek. His dark hair was short and cropped as cut stubble.

"Hello, Ma, here's to you," he said, raising a newly poured Black and White whisky in her direction. "Miss me?"

"Oh, Ted," she said, her voice catching. "I meant to come and see you, really I did, but I found time passing, and before I knew it... "

"I'm glad you didn't." He said, with something of a sneer in his voice. "I'd like to say I was innocent, but we both know I deserved to be in there."

"And you learned your lesson? You'll be a good boy from now on?"

As long as she lived, Ivy never forgot the look Ted shot her in response. Somehow venal, shadowed. Brutal waves hitting the West Pier on a dark day.

"I learned lots of lessons, Ma," he said at last. "None of which you'd like to own. Oh, and by the way, I got places to be, I'm not stopping. Just came to say hello. Can I have another before I'm on my way?"

All the things Ivy wanted to say about new starts and not-too-lates jammed in the roof of her mouth.

As Lesley opened the door, and light flooded the downstairs bar, mother and son stood looking at each other, as if their feet were rooted to the floor. A scene, Lesley recalled later, looking like something from a melodrama.

A Place Where We Belong

The vanity case in the style of a Gladstone bag, all pockmarked leather and scuffs, had obviously once spelled expense. Court snapped its rusted clasp and pulled the sides apart, and clouds of musty-smelling dust shot out. There was a stained magenta moiré lining, rows of tarnished silver-topped bottles, and pots of cold cream, so off as to resemble stilton. Ivory brushes were ravine lined, and had lost bristles along the way.

"Comes wiv a clown's hat." The elderly shop proprietor sniffed, "and the boater. Good hats, once."

Court thought the clown's hat unrecognisable, more like a glue-spotted pancake – and the boater! Someone like Jimmy Edwards must have sat on it. There was air blowing between crown and rim, 'Good hat,' laughed Court, "Whacko! I don't want the hats, ta."

"Few do." The man sighed, giving Court sense that no one wanted the old bloke's merchandise, or entered the shop on Nottingham's Drury Hill, much at all.

Yet, the case drew him, Leichner tubes and greasy carmine sticks staining the bottom, bits of fake moustache, and that backstage odour, somewhere between pan-stick and talc.

55

A sepia calling-card, fixed behind one of the brushes, revealed the corner of an eye and a ludicrously corked brow. Carefully removing the card, Court noted an expansive man in pierrot costume, face all sadness and promised laughter. The signature had turned from blue to lilac, print below reading:

ARCO REGALIA, THE CLOWN PRINCE,
ALWAYS UP TO SOME MONKEY

"Arco Regalia! Never heard of you." Court whispered. A cotton handkerchief marked 'A.R.' was folded behind another brush, and behind that, a note on baby-blue paper:

Dear Peggy, this began, *if this has reached you there's a good chance I am no more, or that the broker's men finally caught-up with me. Sorry about the money and the fish. Always some monkey! Arco.*

Turning, Court laughed to see the old boy at the counter had fallen asleep over a lurid paperback called *Espresso Girls.* The shop and its owner seemed typical of Drury Hill, a climbing street lost to time. Some of the properties were said to date back to the Tudors, and Court, in Nottingham for a meeting at the Royal about next year's panto, couldn't resist a wander past theatrical costumiers and tailors, whose roofs almost touched across the narrow, cobbled street.

Court took his time with the case, looking to see what other gems he'd missed. Unscrewing a pot of cold-cream he was overtaken by a sickly lathery smell, noting a mint imperial lodged at the mess's centre. He quickly re-screwed the lid, re-placing the pot.

"It's like the mummy's tomb, is this, I can't buy it … creepy." He said, to no one in particular. Anyone buying the beast would have a lot of scraping and cleaning-out, that was for sure. There was a small black-silk pom-pom on the case's bottom, presumably the last gasp of Arco's costume, apart from the slaughtered hat. Under this was an address card for:

Miss Peggy Lambert,

Milliner,

26A Lavender Street,

Brighton.

Court wondered what relation Peggy'd been to the Clown Prince? Daughter? ("Regalia" seemed an invented name), Wife? Sister? Lover? Desired one?

As on a silent screen, Court saw the pierrot walking a Brighton street, bunch of roses in outstretched hand. As he reached a milliner's window, the clown paused, gestured, fell to his knees.

ARCO'S IN LOVE read the caption below.

HE'S GOT IT BAD.

The film in Court's head cut to a young woman, framed by the milliner's window. Delicate, with blonde shingled hair, and a chintzy tea-dress.

BUT SHE DOESN'T KNOW IT said the next caption.

Court let his imaginary film unwind – the girl leaving the shop, bustling past the pierrot, whose flowers fell into the gutter.

POOR ARCO!

The screen faded. A ridiculous fantasy, Court realised, as both girl and clown would be long-in-the-tooth by now, if not, as Arco's letter implied, fallen off their twigs. Nothing on the card back, and without knowing why Court slipped it, Arco's calling card, and letter into his pocket. As he left the shop he deposited three shillings in front of the sleeping owner – a shilling an item, not bad takings, he mused.

So why did he feel guilty, as if he'd walked from the shop with the case and all its contents? He'd never stolen so much as a penny chew before, even as a kid. Yet, technically, the items weren't stolen, as he'd left payment.

But what if he'd been seen by a fan, slipping the papers into his pocket: PART OF TV DOUBLE ACT A TEA-LEAF! he could see the headline.

Why hadn't he just bought the case? Why take the papers, they meant nothing to him? And, after all, didn't case and papers belong together?

He should go back, explain to the man and buy the case. It'd be easy, he was only a few streets away, having come down the hill and carried on towards the city centre. The return faded as he strolled. He'd be back in London the following day.

What a few weeks it would be. They'd some promotional gigs for the TV, then appearances at Eastbourne and Brighton, where they were opening a new night-club, *Vimo*'s, on the sea-front. When Court returned to his Nottingham hotel, he took the jacket, folding it into the suitcase, ready for his next travels.

The following few days and travel down South disappeared in a rush of appearances, hand-shakings, and cut ribbons. It was hotter than they thought in Eastbourne, and Brighton much the same. But weather in Brighton, Court always said, could turn on a penny, and the afternoon Billy went home and he stayed on, called for a warmer jacket.

That afternoon, Court was visiting Ivy West at The Cricketers'. Billy now knew she was in Brighton, and Court suspected, with Billy's avoidance of The Cricketers', he knew where. Court had never told him about Ted. What a mess supposedly grown-up lives seemed to be!

After a pint with Ivy, Court fancied a walk. Feeling in his jacket pocket for his cigarette case, fingers brushed against the cards and letter taken from the shop on Drury Hill. "Arco Regalia, I forgot all about you!" Court smiled, wondering he'd ever been so bothered about taking the items. Removing the papers and looking at them, he thought three shillings – what a mug!

There was the Clown Prince, the letter, and the address of Miss Lambert's Lavender Street emporium. "Lavender Street," Court said to himself, "I'm up for a bit of a blow."

Finding Lavender Street would be a release after his afternoon. Ivy had been low, telling of Ted's problems keeping within the law, his stay at Her Majesty's request, and almost immediate going back to old ways on release.

"Billy knows you're here." Court'd said.

"Oh, please don't tell him about Ted, I'd be so ashamed. He'll say I've been an awful mother, and just think I want money off him now he's well-known." Court had made his excuses.

Lavender Street turned out to be elusive, and half empty when you got there. He'd been stopped a few times for autographs on the way, but this area seemed devoid of Brightonian bustle. Court welcomed Brighton for its variety - people seemed to want to talk, and had, even before he was well known. He relished the city's lanes, plus the fact in one night you could end-up chatting to an old film star, young musical hopefuls, and a group of Yorkshire butchers, fire-faced with the promise of dirty weekends.

Turning up Lavender Street, he started to count for number 26A: a restaurant's dark front revealed the usual tiles and checked table-cloths; a tailor's boasted dapper men toiling at pairs of smart trousers; and there were secretive flats with columned doorways. 22A, 22B, 24A, 24B, 26… Not here…

After walking past scrubland between buildings, Court re-traced his steps and counted again. He was right. Between 24B and 28A nothing existed except grass and a lost building's foundation-marks. No Miss Lambert's Millinery Emporium. The rest of the street was well-heeled, so why the scrubland? Bricks and shapes in stone that indicated there'd once been a building, revealed details as Court looked. A mosaic panel was still attached to a bit of wall where the door must have stood, art deco lettering spelling P. L. FOR HATS OF QUALITY.

"Shame I call it, even if it was a bleedin' tragedy, it weren't the building's fault."

Court turned to see a wiry Jack Russell of a man. The shiny suit he sported was built for an even smaller fella. Court thought of that poem *The Rime of the Ancient Mariner*, recited by the monologue artiste, Bransby Williams, where the wedding guest got told a story he didn't want to hear. Court often thought you got to meet shed-loads of Ancient Mariners in one lifetime. Oh, why was he always the wedding guest?

"Really?" he said, trying not to encourage.

"Yeah, council decided to pull it down. 'Cos of what happened. They're going to build some fancy flats, like Brighton needs any more. Got a fag?"

He gave the man a ciggie, hoping it would silence.

"Yeah, that woman who died worked in her shop here for years, and a nice shop it was, too. Hats."

"Oh, well, that's interesting, but…"

"Yeah, got married after years on her own. Some bloke she'd only known for a few months. Women! They said she'd had a husband before, some actor chap, but he'd spent her money and deserted her. She'd a bit of an inheritance and the actor splurged it, that's why she opened the hat shop. Years on her own, making a good living, and then this new chap comes along. She and the actor must've been divorced, 'cos she married this man. Always civil, smiling, he was, but folk round here couldn't take to him."

"What happened?"

"Well, it all seemed to be goin' lovely for them, then, one day, she didn't open the shop. They lived above it, and he hadn't been seen that morning either. There was a big wedding next day, and the matron of honour had come to collect the bridesmaids' hats."

"And?"

"Well, after ages knockin', the matron alerted the neighbours, and everyone grew suspicious. Police were sent for, they broke in, and Bob's yer Uncle." The Mariner took a drag of his fag, and blew out a head of steam. The acridity turned Court's stomach.

"She was dead, wasn't she? Cut up. The 'usband, gone, never seen more. They looked him up but there was no one registered with his name. Some hack at the *Evenin' Argus* found his moniker on an old stone in Saint Nicholas' churchyard. Makes you think."

The Mariner sucked on his fag. "She and the hubby were no spring chickens. Still I'd an idea - told it to police at the time, they said I dreamt it up down the Cricketers'."

Court knew what was coming before the Mariner spoke.

"Remember those suitcase murders during the war? Bloke cut-up lonely women, left them in cases? Small and

Cook, those were two of the girls he killed. Remember their surnames from the papers. Bloke never caught. I reckon the hubby was him. Changed his name, settled down, thought it was all over, then got the urge again, see? Once a killer … and I reckoned him a killer, that smilin' husband none of us ever took to. Police wouldn't have it - but I think I was on to somethin' - he settled down and thought it was all done with, then got the urge."

The Mariner shuffled off, without so much as a goodbye or thanks for the fag.

Court recalled how during the war, his girl Vi'd been so scared about the contents of a case at their digs, he'd had to take it down and have a look. Gazing after the small figure of the Mariner, he thought how Lavender Street had seemed such a lovely name before the Mariner's story had been told.

He turned back to HATS OF QUALITY. A bit of inner wall he hadn't noticed before still maintained its tin-plate sign, showing a woman in a dome-shaped flowered hat, with an attached wedding veil. Standing by her was a man in morning suit, and under them the legend:

BEE-JAY HATS FOR THE MODERN BRIDE

STYLES TAKING US TO

PLACES WE BELONG

Removing cards and letter from his pocket, Court walked across to the poster and dropped the papers to the ground.

"Arco Regalia sent me," he whispered, before walking away, to seek the sea-front's hullaballoo.

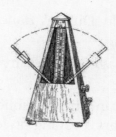

Old Birds

Aggie considered the woman shuffling past The Black Lion, thinking, in a former life, that might have been herself. Had she ever looked so "on the ropes?" She knew she had. Look at that woman! Good scarf, touching you with its bright art deco pattern. Dancers was it? Coral and jade, seemingly the only item clean. It was the old bird's layers, on a heated day, that got to you, coat... cardigan... frock... stranded paste and bright plastic. Not so much plastic as... what did they use to make radios of? *Bakelite*. That was it. See those necklaces, thought Aggie, their chipped-paste told a tale. And pearls, stained like nicotine-edged fingers!

"Poor cow." Aggie said. "I should go over. Stand her a sandwich."

So she opened up, and, going outside, called:

"Ere, love, do you want to come in for a wet or bite to eat? On the house?"

The woman stopped. Blue eyes widened. Orange-hued, lined lips pouted: "Did Mr Middleton send you? Did he call for me? Mr Middleton? Hugo Middleton. He said it likely."

(We've got a right one 'ere, Aggie thought). "No Mr Middleton, love," she replied.

"Oh, well, he'll miss out. I can still do it, you know."

"Still do what?"

63

"Why, the 'Twinkle Dinkle' dance. I'm his 'Twinkle Dinkle Girl'."

"No love. No message. Look, why don't you come in for that sandwich?"

"No thanks. You can't trust publicans, you know, some of them are white-slavers, preying on lonely girls."

"Suit yerself." (And serves me right for asking, Aggie thought).

She let the woman go. Later, Phil said: "I know her, old bird with loads of sparkle round her neck, you know what she does?"

"No."

"Does a circuit. *Lucraft's Bank*, then the *Royal's* Box-Office, and ends-up at *Hannington's* café. Always the same, asks at the bank and theatre if she's wanted, and was message left? In the café, has tea and waves at people. And you offered her a sandwich! She's already short of a couple if you ask me."

"I was once like that, even went to Lucraft's to ask if I still had money there."

"Yes, but *you* were saveable. Gilda knew that. And you had a genuine question. That old biddy's deluded. Dangerous. Thinks she's a young dancing girl. All that stuff about notes, she's waiting for bookings. Calls back!"

"I say that's sad, Phil, not dangerous."

"And I think we've one too many loose on the streets, muttering."

Funny thing, Aggie considered, but after that encounter with the "Twinkle Dinkle Girl", she couldn't seem to walk through Brighton without seeing her. Near the bank, watching a young busker by the Pavilion gates, who managed to get through a few bars of *Please Please Me* before being moved on. Then, outside the Royal gesturing as a doorman informed her she was barred: "You're upsetting custom, Madam," he said, polite but curt, "Dancing that way is an unacceptable manner of approaching a ticket-queue."

"I thought Mr Middleton may be watching," she said, "he might have forgotten my act."

The man indicated no one could forget her act, before going inside and closing the doors.

The woman saw Aggie watching, not recognising her as the person who'd offered food outside The Black Lion.

"Everyone's forgot," she said, sadly. "They'll be sorry on my triumphant return! The Americans may want me. Perhaps the *Folies Bergere*." Then she staggered off.

The woman's similarity to her own might-have-been, disturbed Aggie. When Gilda Graeme had rescued her, Aggie'd been pushing a cart round Brighton's streets. No need to remind *her* of the lonely life, or people's cruelty, as well as goodness that saved. She knew stone beds froze people, and were temporary. Hoping at least. "Miss Twinkle Dinkle" returned to a flat, or crumbling house.

Without Gilda, Aggie might be dead, yet where was Gilda? She'd left Phil... gone away. Years ago. Longer than Aggie cared to remember. No word, or letter, no evening phone-call. Something happened, but Aggie was never sure what. Now she and Phil were married, and she wondered, would Gilda mind? Yes, Gilda Graeme saved her from Miss Twinkle's fate. Aggie with her silent-film past could be wandering The Lanes, muttering.

In fact, Aggie's past caught up with her in remarkable ways, starting with a small cinema in the East Midlands (showing silent films, amongst others) which now regularly received her as guest of honour. She often found herself talking about her early career as "The Kinematograph Girl" and appearing in documentaries, or at galleries using old films for new purposes. Without Gilda it'd still be a barrow in the streets!

One lunchtime, Phil said: "That old bird's become a menace. Ivy at The Cricketers' told me. Miss Twinkle turned-up. Did a weird dance. Started to sing a song, and lifted layers higher than you'd wish. And it's not the first instance, neither, Ivy's barred the woman, and you know Ivy's soft-hearted."

Then, for a few months, sightings ceased. "Maybe she's died, or gone to ground, that dancer-woman."

"In the Laughing Academy more like, bet she's got a new costume with lovely long sleeves."

"Phil, that's not nice!"

"Neither's doing a rude turn in a decent boozer."

Brighton. A busy, warming-up day. Hanningtons heaving with shoppers, seeking distance from sea-front glare. Aggie liked Hannington's; like her, it was a survivor, having been bombed-out and rebuilt; modernised, yet retaining its many-floored charm over several buildings. She sought a new frock for her return to the Midlands cinema, where she'd meet her supporters, Winifred and George again - speaking to an appreciative audience about days spent as the South Coast's silent siren.

She wanted something classy... avoiding "mutton dressed as." An ash-green linen suit caught her eye, above the knee but hardly "mini." Not too low at the front either, with jacket lined in baby-blues.

"The ensemble comes with matching pill-box and scarf in ecru," purred the saleswoman, "the scarf coming free if all items are purchased." Paying up after trying on, then asking to leave boxes at the desk while she continued, Aggie sought treats of coffee and éclair in the café.

She was just settled when she heard commotion. Looking up she saw "The Twinkle Dinkle Girl" fighting off waitress and manager at the queue's edge.

"Mr Middleton might await. I'm costumed. I've been away, you see... a... a rest cure... and I'm sure to have missed his call."

(Rest cure, thought Aggie - Phil was spot on.)

"Twinkle Dinkle" lived-up to her name. Layers were gone; she was spruced. The only item Aggie recognised was the scarf, art deco dancers in jades and corals whirling over an imaginary floor. The costume must have waited years, a bon-bon of a dress, small buttoned boots, and a tricorn, pom-pom festooned hat.

The spectacle made Aggie want to cry.

"Not girlish, ghoulish," Phil would've said. He'd have been right, of course.

But some forgotten melody pulled Aggie's heartstrings as she looked at the disturbance, as the lobster-hued manager went for store security.

"You informed me there was no seat," Twinkle Dinkle said to the waitress, "but there's clearly a table."

"Oh, no, Madam, that's reserved. Mrs Costain... late luncheon."

"You made her up, I don't believe you. You just don't like theatricals."

"We can assure you, Madam, Mrs Costain's shopping. And she's in the music business."

"Well, you don't like dressed-up theatricals, then."

Rising, Aggie could stand no more. Closing in, she had a greater focus on Miss Twinkle's get-up. From further away, the costume just looked inappropriate. The closer, the more realisation dawned; here was a young girl's frock deposited on a haggard frame.

Orange-sateen bodice was topped by puff sleeves, and wire-enforced, shortened crinoline shone with those pom-poms decorating her tricorn. Boots revealed scrawny legs, and the effect of crinoline-wiring was to display lemon-sateen pantaloons.

"Leave it," Phil would've said, but one glance at apricot blush on Miss T's wrinkly-monkey face told Aggie she couldn't.

"Excuse me," she said to the waitress, "I know this lady by sight, and I'm seated at a table for two. I don't mind if she joins me," and she indicated the table. "If she will, I don't think you'll have need of that security man."

The old woman swung skirts and began: "Twinkle dinkle do, a twinkle de, a twinkle do, I'll be the girl for you."

Aggie touched her arm: "Come on, here's a seat. What do you want? Coffee?"

"Yes. Will, Mr Middleton be coming?"

"No. I think it's his day off."

"Oh."

The woman plonked down.

"What's your name? Your real name? I can't call you Twinkle. I'm Aggie."

"Flo."

"Well, Flo, I think we should have coffee then leave. I'll walk you home. Mr Middleton's clearly stood you up."

68

In the distance, manager, waitress, and security man argued.

Then, the waitress left, nearing the empty table. Aggie heard her speak – soft, placatory, impressed. The manager ushered in a smart blonde in cream suit. The suit was Chanel, Aggie was sure, type in all the magazines. That tailored woman (whose smart pill-box atop blonde French-pleat looked salon-fixed) didn't register anything odd about Miss Twinkle – despite most of the café staring fit to bust. She must have extraordinary self-possession not to gawp, Aggie thought.

Another look saw Aggie forget all about Miss Twinkle, Hannington's and her waiting shopping. "Mrs Costain," said the waitress, "we're ever so excited about the *New Beat* tour coming here." The girl's freckly face flushed under her white cap.

"Thank you," crooned the woman through perfect orchid lipstick.

The manager bent low, asking: "Madam, do you mind if the store photographer comes for a few snaps, before you leave?"

"My pleasure."

Aggie stared - if the woman recognised her, no flicker crossed her face. Blonde hair, fresh style, but right features, cherubic lips, and beauty mark.

"Oh Gilda," Aggie said: "how could you not acknowledge me?"

"I'm not Gilda, dear, I'm Flo," said the vision in orange opposite. "Surely you've not forgotten already! You must be losing the plot."

69

BRAND NEW BEAT

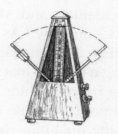

Enchanted Evenings

Brighton, one of the first gigs of the *New Beat* tour from the United States, had seen the woman who was once Gilda Graeme, nervy.

Not that she called herself Gilda anymore, but Ava Costain – 'Mrs Nathan Costain' when being arsey. Costain as she'd taken Nathan's surname at last, marrying in Williamsburg, New York State, when she was certain Jacky Boy Simms, husband number two, was dead. Husband number one, Bollock-Headed Lionel, she hardly thought about.

Ava, because *Pandora and the Flying Dutchman*, starring Ava Gardner, was her favourite film despite the new wave. Two hubbies, both meeting various makers, the first maybe upstairs, the second almost certainly in the heated basement. And now number three, younger than her, of a different race to her, and certainly better looking than her or any individual she'd ever met. Could be the plot of a film, starring Ava Gardner, she thought.

Good job she'd chosen Ava and not Pandora! A Pandora running a modern music show in her husband's absence would never do. Sounded like a lady novelist in lilac! Still, new name or no, she hadn't been sure about coming back.

Phil, her ex-beau, had a hand in Jacky's death, she was sure. It had been unproved that the young man's drowning was anything but accidental, and she'd sworn the body she'd seen wasn't Jacky's anyway. As Jacky wasn't officially marked as dead, Nathan had managed to get some fake papers for her, omitting a second marriage, and they'd been married an ocean away from Brighton. In the US she'd been down as Ava Grahame from the off, consigning Gilda Simms or Graeme to the dust-bin. Maybe the fake papers meant she and Nathan weren't really hitched, it was a grey area.

And what did it matter whether she was in fact, Mrs Costain, or not? She was a born liar, suspecting it was one aspect of her personality Nathan was attracted to.

She thought of Jacky Boy's tattoo, an inky version of her pout, and shuddered. What she'd looked at in the morgue wasn't him, just an empty house. The lie didn't count. Still, having someone drowned made Phil beyond the pale... she'd sworn never to acknowledge him any more... and if that meant abandoning her friend Aggie too, then so be it.

On the grapevine (otherwise known as Courtney Cooper, to whom she'd foolishly written in an off-guard moment) she'd heard Aggie and Phil were hitched, and why not? She'd been Stateside years, working with Nathan on his musical projects from a small office in Bedford Falls, upstate New York - and while it wasn't, by a long stretch, "The Motor City", music put together there was fresh and gaining ground. In fact, of late, it had unexpectedly gained so much ground from rising up several billboards, they'd moved to New York City – leaving the Bedford Falls office in the hands of a manager, Mr Angel.

"Of course," someone from a big label commented at an industry gathering at the *Hilton*, "you're still 'Race Records' under another name, no matter how many platters you sell."

"Times are changin'" said Nathan, grinning despite narrowed eyes.

"Not in the South. Besides, in spite of Mrs Costain's 'charms', the black audience is where your sales are. Best build on that. White audiences won't get it, and expect a heap of trouble should even your city audience be too mixed."

"In New York? Absurd! They get us here."

"At some venues, sure. But don't let that fool you, scratch a so-called cool-nik, and you'll find a conservative at heart. I met a 'poet' the other day, angry young man, played the African drums... a boy whiter than me. Said all sorts of things about a mixed society. I happen to know his Daddy runs a soft drinks company whose major buyers are the Southern States. He's angry now, but when that inheritance comes a-knockin', Sonny Jim will put drums away and toe the line like the rest of them."

Nathan had fumed in the cab on the way back. He'd had one further shot for the executive, whose grey suit and slick hair masked an adder's smile:

"We have one mixed audience waiting for us. They love our music and are just kids wanting to dance."

"Oh yeah, and where are this mythic, integrated crowd?"

"England. We're planning a tour. You know, where my wife comes from, with her 'charms'. We get their invasion, well, now, they get ours."

"Good luck with that, Boy. The Beatles have our plush hotels and diners, you get small venues, cold taps, and outside johns. You won't make enough money for the fare home."

"We'll see. I bet you one hundred dollars it'll be a hit."

"Double it. Oh, and, Mr Costain, I'll buy you out and produce some great 'race records' for our label - when Daddy comes crawling home."

Ava knew, vile as the man's manner was, he had a point. America meant limits for them. Due to chiefly black acts, touring the South was only possible in "colored areas", or at white venues where the acts came in by the back door, used different bathrooms, and were accommodated way, way out of town.

If they booked white venues, black audiences didn't get to see them. If they booked "colored only" bars, white venues refused to host them in the same month, and takings were low. Then there was the spectacle of herself and Nathan holding hands as man and wife. They had to enter by back doors, and she could sit in seats where he could not. They tried leaving the plane together when they'd arrived for their first experiment of a Southern tour, the venues chiefly white, the crowd turning up to greet them separated into different aisles. There was trouble now, stirrings and protests, and so there bloody should be, she thought.

She'd had to get straight back on the plane for New York, being jeered, booed, and spat at just for being Nathan's other-half. "Go home, bitch, you're a traitor to your race," a young red-faced woman in pointed-glasses screamed.

"Go home, before we kill you in your shameful bed," cried her equally deranged mother.

Nathan insisted she return: 'no gal of mine's being intimidated by such ugly females.' He'd said.

Even if acceptance in New York was only one layer deep, at least it was a layer. As records grew in popularity, show business papers tried to be positive without offending more conservative readers:

MR AND MRS COSTAIN – A VARIED MATCH

LOVE WINS OVER COLOR

It sounded like bad jokes to her, and she didn't want to know what papers favoured by the men in hooded uniforms said.

The British tour would be a relief, despite her having to avoid Aggie and Phil when getting to Brighton. Nathan was staying home for the first leg, sorting recording deals and contracts, until the tour's last dates, when they hit Brighton, then London, for a second time – then he'd be joining them to see how she'd done.

"Me, your representative abroad," she'd said, "you must trust me, Mr Costain."

Now, his representative had seen the first Brighton gigs, and they'd moved on. Scanning the mirror, on her first night in London, the woman staring back from the hotel bedroom, bore little relation to her old self. Blonde hair, salon-sculpted into a style far removed from Rita Hayworth curls – but, hadn't Orson Welles made Hayworth, then his wife, cut and bleach red tresses for *Lady from Shanghai*? Ava considered Welles and Costain to have much in common, both enigmatic, good looking men, who knew what they wanted, and screw the system.

Except the system seemed to be eating Mr Welles alive from what she could see: *Touch of Evil* had been masterful, but that beautiful man seemed to have become a malevolent bullfrog of an actor. She wondered if America's big labels would do as much for Nathan, didn't want to see him

77

producing brilliance in the face of crass, only to have crass organise the distribution.

In the mirror, make-up was faultless and of the moment, pale pink lips, light skin, and dark many-lashed eyes. Her scandalously-priced suit was pure Jackie Kennedy, cream boucle blending with oatmeal and gilt furnishings of her room. She was staying at the best all the way, as were the headliners.

"We have to spend darlin', we can't look cheap. Cheap can be some of us on the road, but not you – it would imply we were a label *not* goin' places. My stars have to look like stars from the get-go, and management? Who'd you get to meet in a boarding house?"

He was right, of course, but they were already way in the red. On the dressing table, Nathan's photo shone from its silvered frame. Nat King Cole features and patent waved hair still seemed miraculous to her. "I'm counting on you'" the message below read. "I'll do my best, Lover Boy," she whispered.

It had come as a shock when Aggie recognised her that first day in Brighton. Over weeks she'd conned herself that she was utterly transformed. Bloody hell, her inner voice had whispered, that girl never did miss a trick.

Aggie'd been seated at a table in Hannington's café, with some old bird got up like a fruit salad. She'd looked straight at her, winced, and whispered something involving Ava's old name. "Crapola" as Nathan would say. Gilda, or as Mrs Costain reminded herself, "Ava", ignored her, picking at a salad and letting Aggie and her companion leave before rising to go herself.

It had bothered her, sure, but not that much. The tour was on and she had bigger fish to fry if they were going to make waves, and allow Nathan to throw dollars in that smug executive's face.

Brighton gigs had gone well. Folk were appreciative, now word had travelled and they were to appear on *Ready Steady Go!* to promote later gigs. Nathan left a message at the hotel to say someone had got-wind of *Ready Steady* in the States and gifted them *Shindig!* on their return – maybe Mr Costain had a magic touch for others like he did for her.

At Brighton's clubs, young modernists, keen to hear live what they'd only experienced on record, queued for acts and merchandise. Often, they clutched boxes of treasured single-sleeves with them, the vinyl at home lest it broke, to be signed at the stage-door. They made Ava smile, dancing with serious faces, the boys in immaculate suits or pants and Italian sweaters, girls in short skirts and winkle-picker shoes.

Acts were beyond slick, and happy not to have to enter hotels by the back door. Men in fondant tuxedos, like Big Webbly Jones, moved with grace and fervour. The Delmonts... Little Carmen and the Toreadors... names and moves to conjure with.

The fans were hooked. Brighton had been fine. But smaller Northern and East Midlands towns? Who knew?

The modernists were individuals of devotion. Saved programmes, tickets, anything Big Webbly threw into the crowd. Dancing with concentration, often staring at polished or brushed shoes. Sure, there'd be other types of fan, but these were Nathan's faithful. Ava wondered what black performers' music said to them, what Bedford Falls and New York City produced that animated accountants' clerks and girls from shoe stores? Nathan said it was the beat, pure and simple, a beat giving them back their heart and soul.

It had come as a surprise to her, how much she'd come to love the music – the bounce and strut, the defiance of "I may be broken hearted but my sorrow has class," exuding every note. "I look in the mirror and what do I see?/My cheatin' baby, looking back down at me," Big Webbly bawled. Trite words that, siphoned through his gravel tones, became love letters from a jail cell.

Their *New Beat* tour was organised like a military campaign, every angle covered. She still marvelled how these tours didn't follow logical patterns across the land. Sure, they began with Brighton and London, but then moved far North, West Midlands, North again, East Midlands, South, North, South. She recognised by the time Nathan joined at the tour's end, they'd know if they'd made enough cash and conquered enough hearts to do it again. Pity he wasn't arriving earlier, she thought, as his cashmere camel coat and champagne style would add sparkle.

"I miss you," she said down the phone from her hotel.

"Me too, Baby, me too."

"How are things?"

"Well, I can sign Big W to Come Clean Records in London, they're a small outfit, but goin' places. I may be arriving sooner than we said, so we don't miss a trick with that one. They may get us The Marquee Club, you know, Soho, Wardour Street, so the guy said. I'm changing Big to Ronophone here – they've had the guts just to say 'music' so he wouldn't be just regarded as a niche 'race' recording. That company I talked to down South turned out to be a man and canine outfit – I dropped them, no regrets either side, Baby."

She told him about gigs, trying to paint for him the queuing modernists, record sleeves in their believers' hands. Just before putting the phone down, she added:

"At the last one, this girl came up to me, you would have liked her, Nathan. She had a navy blue dress with a red collar, and bright auburn hair cut very short. Anyway, she came up and asked if I was Mrs Ava Costain. I said yes, and she had a picture of us in her pocket, cut from a paper, then coloured by hand with bright paints and stuck onto card. She said she was studying to be an artist, and would I sign it? I did, and she told me it was going to be part of a big music collage.

"It's called 'Enchanted Evenings' she said, 'because that's what you and Mr Costain give us, enchanted evenings.' Then she left, and, as I watched her go I thought I hoped I got to see her work in a big gallery some day."

"Enchanted Evenings," said Nathan, his voice growing faint with the line's crackle. "I like that. Maybe we should re-name the tour. Or at least the final gig. Ava, can you hear me? Are you still there, Baby?"

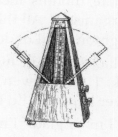

Brushes with Pop

"Hello, Mrs Costain, remember me? I got you to sign that photograph?"

Ava did recall the girl giving her a candy-coloured *homage* to herself and Nathan, in Brighton a few weeks back. Now, at the last London gig before moving on to Sheffield, she stood before Ava in new guise – once flame hair so ash blonde as to now be almost blue.

"Hope you don't mind," the girl continued, "but I had something to give you." She dug through the dolly-bag shaped pocket of her orange dress, producing a small, white invitation:

BRUSHES WITH POP

STELLA BAX AND FRIENDS INVITE YOU

TO THEIR PRIVATE VIEW OF

AN EXHIBITION AT THE BOTY GALLERY

it read, with date and promise of wine following.

"Stella Bax, that's me," said the girl, "Might you come? Only I'm displaying 'Enchanted Evenings', you know, the collage you're in."

Ava looked at the date, months ahead... She had to hand it to her, the girl was organised. All this and new hair in the short time between Brighton and London.

"Well, actually Stella, you're in luck. That date fits in with when we're back, I might even be able to bring Mr Costain along. Whatever happens, I'd love to come."

The girl beamed. "I'm so glad. I'm still working on my pieces, but there's ages yet. And, really, I've been very lucky. I've not quite left college and I've already got a London agent, a few of us have. I'm down here lots, these days."

"Well," said Ava, "if you want some advice from someone who's been around (which you probably don't) make sure your management treats you right, and if not, dump them like shit off a shovel."

The girl laughed: "My Mam used to say that," she said, betraying hint of a Northern accent.

"Your Mum must be proud, you getting on so well in the art world."

The girl looked hard at her. "Mam died last year, she got run over by a lorry. She saw someone she knew and ran across the road without looking. Ours was a quiet town, you never hardly saw a lorry."

"I'm sorry. Well, your Dad, then?"

"He doesn't speak to me. Not since I got a bursary for art school, and he says I changed my accent n'all. He wanted me to go to secretarial college, see. Said art schools were for rich boys. He wasn't speaking to Mum, either, when she had her accident. Kept saying she was running across the road to meet a fella."

"From the sound of your Dad, I don't blame her," said Ava in her forthright manner, then: "Sorry, Love."

"You're all right. He blames me for her accident. Said if I hadn't gone she wouldn't have taken up with a fella. That I gave her ideas. He let me go to the funeral, but wouldn't have me back to our house. Sorry, I don't know why I'm telling you this."

"I've got that kind of face. Stella, you're young to be going it alone, and so was I. My parents were mad as a box of frogs, as it happens. But just think, here I am, though I wouldn't claim it's been easy."

The girl looked at her Mary-Jane shoes. "People have been very kind." She said.

"Well, that's all right, but if you include boys in that statement, remember some are nice, while some are nice to get into your knickers."

The girl laughed. "I'll try and remember that."

"Stella," said Ava, "send me a few of your flyers for the show, and I'll make sure I pass them on to some good people. You can send them to the hotel I'm next at, I'll give you a card with the address."

"No need, I have some in my bag, but I will give you my card, it's got one of my images on."

Ava watched Stella Bax move through the hipster crowd. Something slight about her frame made her a kiddy's ghost. Ashy blonde added to pallor highlighted by the orange dress. Not known for her maternal leanings, nevertheless, Ava felt a pang.

As it happened, Ava saw Stella again the following day. As Ava was overseeing the loading of a van full of equipment and lesser acts, the girl was walking past, armed with a medium-sized canvas wrapped in brown paper. A pale blue coat and shoes made her more-ghostly than ever. Ava was about to shout her over, but a privacy in the girl's expression stopped her short – that type of concentration that sealed her from everything going on.

"That girl'll hit headlines for art, all right, and then for every wrong reason."

The thought came unbidden, Ava wishing it had never occurred. It was soon overtaken by a mix-up over guitars, and various people having maps showing conflicting routes. A few weeks into the first Northern part of the tour, and audiences proved larger than hoped for. One Sunday morning, Ava saw hint of Stella's progress in a glossy weekend magazine. It was an article titled: "Ones to Watch – A Very British Invasion", with Stella being the only female listed in a catalogue of male artists. The section on her read:

While Mr Peter Blake turns to Elvis and Cliff for inspiration, and others create concepts at their most abstract, Miss Stella Bax is ploughing her own furrow in the competitive and often very male world of British art.

A 'modernist' in the popular music sense of the term, she is obsessed with the New Beat Tour organised by Mr Nathan Costain and currently hitting these shores from America. Miss Bax's collages feature Mr Costain, his wife Ava, and performers such as singers Big Webbly Jones and Little Carmen and her Toreadors.

Truly, Miss Bax appears a talent worth watching. Seen holding a picture based on Mrs Costain and her husband aboard an internal American flight, she is unrepentantly 'for' this fresh popular music.

Have a look at her work, and at the forthcoming Boty Gallery exhibition, and, who knows, you might be 'for' it too!

The article finished with both exhibition, and some of the later Southern tour dates. Publicity, Ava knew, you couldn't buy.

It was still shocking to see her name in print as "Ava". Internally, she remained Gilda, but realised the name she'd held onto all through the war was now dead as Jacky Boy.

A voice inside made her hope Stella Bax remained Stella Bax, no matter what her hair colour became.

Tickets to Ride

"What's he called?"

"Big Webbly Jones."

"So, he's a fat man act?"

"No, Billy, he's a singer, one of the new kind, over from the States. He's on with Little Carmen and the Toreadors."

"Acrobats?"

"Now you're just being facetious, Bill. Thing is, they've sent us free tickets to their show being filmed. Want us to be part of it."

"How come?"

"Because, well, partly because, I know their management – Mrs Costain – not that I knew her under that name."

"Oh, very cloak-and-dagger, did you 'know' her in the over-familiar sense?"

"No, just mates. More fool me, she was lovely. Anyhow, their show's being filmed at the A. R. studios, not our lot, but the Beeb are keen for us to do it."

"Why?"

"Because it's seen as the 'young idea.' They've been on *Ready Steady Go!* and now a new show, *Pop It!* from the same

89

stable, wants them. Said it would be great if we were on, to demonstrate we're not past it, that we're invited to the party. The Beeb think it would be good for our 'profile', bring us younger fans."

"What, ancient coves like us, down among the hipsters? I think that's what they call them."

"Well, kids may like us. Besides, for the show it's like gettin' the nod from the older generation, Mrs Costain would count it a favour."

"And we can't let the lady down."

Billy wasn't convinced. A load of twisting and gyrating kids with them looking on in their suits. He could see why the studio thought they should go, but really, should they? Common sense was voting it a "miss." He recalled some of the old acts, last gasp of the Victorian halls as he thought of them, struggling to make it new and survive, both during and after wartime. Oddly perhaps, some of them had done better during the war, as ENSA needed material no matter how old-hat, and only a few acts, like himself and Courtney were younger but invalided out.

It was "after" when some struggled, with spangled costumes and songs containing phrases like "spooning with my girl", or ventriloquists who looked older than their crumbling dummies. Some acts had seen sense, if unable to move with the times, and joined *Thanks for the Memory* type shows. These could be profitable, but only if, in old age, you were prepared to move from place to place like you had as a nipper – a few performers had recently died on the road.

Billy considered the Mighty Rosco, still working as a pot-boy at Yates's Wine Lodge in Nottingham, who'd been offered a few *Thanks for the Memory* style gigs, and had turned these down. "I'm settled in Notts, and I'm not snuffing it on stage, or being carried on in a bloody chair," he'd told Grandwem. "If I died in the dressing room I'm that small they might not find me until they packed-up, maybe not even then. No, I had a grand innings, and that'll do. Let them remember the best of me."

Rosco had a point, and unlike some, an income and a roof. Still, those doing *Thanks for the Memory* were lucky – unlike people Billy witnessed trying to beg entry into managers' offices, or besieging TV companies with inappropriate letters; these individuals could break your heart, he thought.

He and Court sometimes received letters themselves, some from people whose work they'd known, but often from those with tenuous connections to their variety careers. "We met in..." and "You may not remember coming across me, but..." were openers to dread. Worst were letters from folk they'd never heard spoken of, bottom of the bill, or doing fillers at nudie shows. Some of these, you suspected, hadn't been in work for years, and harked back to juvenile careers, cut short by war or personal tragedy. "The Boys Most Likely To," tried not to send money, but occasionally weakened. "We may be suckers, but it could be us," Court would say. Letters of gratitude that came back were often unbearable.

"Some of them are so un-billable as to be near amateur," Court once remarked, "in fact, that's not fair on amateurs. You get some great performers in rep or am-drams." Billy had to agree.

Still, there was a recent spate of letters that had spelled "amateur," which worried them both. A slew of pale blue, Izal-thin envelopes, from someone signing himself "Gin Pride – Pride of the House" whose catch line "Gin's a

Tonic'" was printed as a letterhead by means of, what looked like, a child's John-Bull printing outfit.

Dear Messrs Cooper and Bean, one missive began, *how heartening to see a double-act doing so well on the box. It gives hope to we in the profession who cannot be counted so fortunate.*

In juvenile days, when I came on as a "filler" between film reels at the picture houses, I was, as you may know, also regarded as a "boy most likely to." Yet, adult disappointments, and a career halted by war, made valued bookings hard to come by.

I have, of late, decided to try and re-kindle my early promise, and begin again. At present, I reside at Bexhill-on-Sea, but am looking further afield, even to the land of television, for my re-start. I perform once weekly at Rapelli's Trattoria, as management considered an act may give their evening dining an edge over competitors. I also hone my routine at several old folks' homes in the area, although, thus far, on a voluntary basis.

"Poor sods," said Court, "captive audience in every sense."

"Be kind!"

Billy continued reading the letter, his favourable demeanour changing with every new sentence:

"Listen to this, Court!"

I am a grafter by nature, and prepared to entertain any place offering me a booking, to get a hand-up. To come to it, gents, being that you've become so awful high-and-mighty, and on the televisual screen, I was wondering if you might see your way to including me in one of your shows, on either stage or box.

"You think he's being rude with 'high-and-mighty', Bill, he may not mean it, that might be an unfortunate turn-of-phrase. And he says he's a grafter."

"Yes? Well, there's more. More than an unfortunate phrase here! He goes on – "

92

I'm 'Gin-and-Tonic' to my admirers, and 'Gin-and-It' to many girls. If you haven't 'room for a small one,' as the saying goes, I'm wondering if you could see your way to financing a small show of mine with guaranteed returns, called Gin and Bare It. *This is a risqué script, that those who've read count most droll. Perhaps I'll come and see you, and we'll agree terms.*

"A bit previous, Bill, but you can't fault the lad for trying."

By the way, Billy read, heatedly, ignoring Court, *I garner the strength to ask for funds, from the notion that you're known to help others in our most competitive profession. I understand, Mr Bean, your niece, Miss P, is doing nicely designing costumes for shows. I assume that her rise is partly down to your endeavours.*

"Cheeky arse!"

"There's more. But how does he know Beryl's my niece, she's always gone under the name of Potter?"

"People know, Bill. Everyone knows."

"Yes, people in the business. But I've never come across this Herbert? Have you?"

Court shook his head, and together they finished reading the letter, which concluded *I assume that helping someone rise is not just limited to family, yours in expectation…*

"Expectation of a clip 'round the lug-hole." Billy snorted.

In calmer mood, they decided not to reply to Mr Gin. Their silence was met, within a few days, with a barrage of Izal-weedy envelopes all in the same type-written form, with John Bull letterhead. The post continued for three weeks, growing increasingly sharp, the last letter being particularly unpleasant in tone:

Dear Messrs Cooper and Bean. You seem to decline replying to your postbag. To what end I do not know. I have been polite and industrious in my pleas for either work or funding. I do not ask aid, but employment. I presume you are more used to fan-mail. I can only conclude that you have become too grand or busy for the likes of I.

"Traditional 'red melodrama underlining', nice," said Court.

I see that Miss P's career continues to flourish. Whilst those of us not party to your stellar-orbit languish. I shall however decline to take offence, and await your summons. Perhaps one day I will turn up at the studios and surprise both of you with my wit and erudition! Then you shall regard what talent you are turning down. Or, it might only take a visit to Rapelli's of Bexhill to amend your folly. Otherwise I may seek you out!

The letter worried "Messrs Cooper and Bean" enough to show their studio manager.

"Nutters," he said, "our world's full of them. Get your mug on the telly and they all come out of the bleeding woodwork. Even the man who reads the news gets love letters, some of them quite blue. Say he's 'their awaited soul-mate', nutters! This one's probably harmless, they often feel safe at a distance. Most don't travel. Still, I'll get security and the doormen not to let in anyone we don't know. I can see this bloke, smell him, even. Some cologne for men they haven't made in ten years, and pipe smoke. I know what he looks like without meeting the bastard."

So, Court thought, could he. A wiry individual, with penchants for suits too short in the legs or long beige overcoats. He probably wore bow ties and had pencil parted hair with pomade. Oh, and one of those nosebleed moustaches, that strange men sported without notion it gave them an air of Hitler.

Yes, anyone like that petitioning the studio door, would be given the right bum's rush.

In the meantime, Court and Billy were due at a studio across town, as Billy had been persuaded *Pop It!* would be good for them.

"Now, all you have to do, Gents," said the Floor Manager, "is stand by on the spot we've marked, tap your feet, and look as though you're enjoying the music. We'd recommend not dancing, no offense, but a few weeks ago, someone from a popular quiz tried it, and... well... he made himself look like a berserk windmill."

"But we do dance," said Billy, offended.

"Yes, but tap, not this modernist stuff. Best left to the young, in my book. Now remember, smile, on the spot, tap toes, lovely."

"Shows we get it, but we're not trying to be teenagers," said Court.

"Exactly, that's the stuff."

"Max Miller wouldn't have done this," said Billy under his breath.

"Yeah, he would, did *The Market Song* with Lonnie Donegan. Now behave, or they'll throw us out."

"So," said Court to the manager (looking around the Op-art set with its raised Go-go plinths, and specially erected fake bar with a sign saying CLUB, where they were to stand) "where are your dancers from?"

"Oh, chiefly from the *New Beat* tour, with a few of our own, and some from a local club. We had a raffle for tickets. Some of the kids had heard of you."

"A raffle? Now *that's* old fashioned," Court beamed.

The kids were cool, draped in clothes and make-up especially constructed for black-and-white. A few older people, clearly actors, unmentioned by the manager, were kitted-out as "eccentrics," a comic golfer and chef, for what reason Court and Billy couldn't figure. Girls had short skirts, huge disc earrings, and plastic boots. Lads sported suits or "modernist" sweaters and two-tone shoes. "Way out means smart," laughed Billy.

A pre-filming warm-up began, first up was Big Webbly Jones, who sang with the burning gusto of old blues singers, the beat might be new, Court thought, but Paul Robeson tones would never go out of style. Filming after warm-ups was live and the dancers had to go on for as long as the act lasted. Like the acts, dancers got a short run-through, being bellowed at to "go, really go," and "let their hair down." 'Let's see the eccentrics," bellowed the director, whose beard made him look like a fifteen-year-old in costume.

It was then that something extraordinary happened. From behind the chef, a man emerged in a suit that was much too small for his spindly frame. He danced, if that was the right word, by throwing his body forward and jerking arms in the air. The record playing to provide a beat was *Ticket to Ride*, although this would be replaced by something from the tour for the actual recording. Occasionally, when the phrase 'ticket to ride' was repeated, the man pointed at Billy and Court, hissing: "Gin, gin's the thing." Before spiralling away.

"Who, by my sainted arse, is that?"

The floor manager was beside himself.

"I said eccentrics, not the criminally insane!" said the director.

"Search me who he is, I didn't see him get on set. We had a chef and a comedy golfer, I don't know what he's supposed to be got up as," said a young man wearing headphones.

"He squeezed between us when we came in," a girl in a tartan skirt was explaining, "We thought he was one of the funnies, he had a ticket."

"Right," the floor manager yelled in the man's direction, "let's see that pissing ticket."

The cringing man dug in his pocket, producing a tattered square of blue card. "Eat at Rapelli's," the Manager read, "the only night out with free Gin-and-Tonic. What?"

"That's me, Gin, that's my act... Gin's a tonic?"

"Is it? Anyone know this, this, time-waster?"

Court almost said "yes," but concluded it would look bad for them, and wouldn't help Gin, either. "Never ask oldies," they'd say, "they come with creepy followers."

"Right." The Manager had the man by his thin collar. "Out, now, and if we see you here, or at any TV studio again, there'll be a prosecution."

"But I just wanted..."

"OUT!"

At this point, a braided commissionaire appeared, to lead the shamed Gin from the building. As Gin was led away, he turned and fixed his eye on Court and Billy. The malice in his gaze making Billy shudder.

"Well, that's today's excitement over, Ladies and Gents, as you were," the manager yelled.

"Just what I thought," Court spoke aloud, addressing no one in particular, "Apart from the coat, I was bang-on. Right down to the Hitler 'tache. Well, well, let's hope we've seen the last of him."

MANSFIELD'S SMALL FACES

Changelings

Shirl scribbled in her pink diary with the blue clasp. Printed dates vanished under jet ink. Words came fast, none of them right ones for the day she'd had. Questions she'd forgotten how to answer crowded and got crossed-out – how old was Grandwem? Younger than they thought, and she looked? She was Grandwem to them all, even to Shirl, her remaining daughter, even to George, her husband (sometimes Win, but not often). What was Bem Bean, Shirl's Dad, and Grandwem's first hubby really like? Why when she re-married had she kept his surname? And what did any of it matter, really, after the day's events?

Shirl was scribbling for Little Rita, so if anything happened to her or Alf, Rita would grow-up knowing her Mam's thoughts... Not like Beryl when their first Rita died, growing up piecing recollections as best she could, aided by Shirl, Alf, Billy, George, and Grandwem.

Paper was tear-sploshed, lines blurring. Shirl hadn't even realised she was crying. Putting pen down, she wiped a hand across her hot face. She could hear the baby cooing in the next room as Alf sang to her: "I fell in love with Mary from the Dairy, but Mary wouldn't fall in love with me."

The baby laughed, or seemed to. Then he began a more modern song, whose words Shirl couldn't place. Little Rita bawled. Alf returned to Max Miller, which she seemed to like best. Cooing began again.

Rita only home a few weeks, Beryl back at work and getting used to her routine, and this had to go and happen! Shirl looked back at the page where she'd begun to write:

The Car/avan. We foun/d. This Mo/rning.

All phrases with bloody great pen-lines through. Nothing seemed right and all was crossed-out until she'd steeled herself, and written it down just as things happened. She'd got as far as that morning's events. Maybe that was it for now. Although she knew this was one story she had to return to.

From outside, familiar sounds of George seeking the outdoor lavvy. True, he and Win now had a grand new one put in the extended and freshly done bathroom upstairs, as had she and Alf. But George was resolute in his adherence to what he called "old faithful," and, like Norrie, preferred a tin bath before the fire once a week, rather than what Norrie termed "the iniquity of bathing next to the thunder-box." Shirl realised she knew the symphony of George's routine by heart:

Click, door opening.

Click, snap... Door shut and locked.

Sounds of someone lowering themselves, then sitting.

Rustle... Rustle...

Newspaper being taken from under a fair-isle tank-top, and spread out so the front page could be read.

Then "Salleee... Salleee... Never, never wander, away from the alleee and meeee... "

Or, whistling of *Colonel Bogey* which Win's budgie would hear from the kitchen, joining in.

"Salleee… Salleee… Win! There's no Izal."

"No, you lot waste it, I've cut up some magazines and strung them next to the seat."

"I'm not wiping me sen on *The People's Friend*! Anyway, we can afford toilet roll, your son's on television, and there's not a war on."

"I'll have a look for some under the sink."

Shirl considered new bathrooms gracing their houses in matching milkshake pinks. Sinks shaped like shells with dolphin-held soap dishes. Toilets that complimented sink and bath with proper roll-holders. Billy had given them the money a few weeks ago saying, "No niece of mine's going to bath in a bowl in the sink, besides, the ewd uns could do with a good spring-clean." Men had come and fitted stuff soon after. Bevelled mirrors were a sight to behold! They'd had lavs inside and out for a few years, but not these, the *princes* of lavs!

"I'm not using that lav, or coming to borrow a bath, they're too swank-pot. Stains'd spoil," said Norrie.

George had nodded approval.

"Well my arse deserves the best,' said Alf, 'I'm not stinting."

Norrie wouldn't ever use it. He'd grumbled down the garden for a fortnight, using his weekly visit as a platform for extolling a tin bath's virtues. "I live in a caravan, and mek a fire to have mine outside, lovely!"

"What about winter?"

"I conserves meself, to keep the warm in."

103

Shirl could see his bent figure now, shuffling down the path, *Racing Times* under his arm to use as paper. Increasingly smaller, she noted, snowy hair, string-tied moleskin trousers, and collarless shirt topped by a cornflower-spotted neckerchief. Of late, he'd brought Peggy (tame owl perched on his arm, white and beige feathers seeming an extension of her master's hair). One of his dogs also followed, sometimes a pup, often wearing a neckerchief, too. Owl and dog would wait, Peggy on the roof-edge, pup at the door, until Norrie came out.

"Look at it, like bleddy *Zoo Quest*," said Alf.

In truth, dogs always followed Norrie. Mostly his own, though sometimes a mongrel would catch wind of him, trailing him down the street. Often he'd arrive with one, saying, "This lass followed me into town, reckon she's a keeper." He knew when a dog had an owner, and turned up at doors with, "I believe this to be yours." How he got the addresses was a mystery. Once, he took back an all-sorts hound, one ear raised, and one flat, to be greeted by a small girl who said, "Why have you bought that dog back? It's fair a bloody gump."

What would dogs and pups do now? Shirl had a vision of them, from borzoi to scrap of terrier, howling round Norrie's caravan. They couldn't be got rid of, homes would have to be found. Then there was the owl and... that didn't include the new litter Win had brought home to feed, not so much dogs, more mewling rodents. Win would insist the runt be kept, and it looked a right bloody gump n'all.

But... Shirl was being previous, ahead of the story she'd written. She stared at her words as if they were a stranger's: *Morning Story* the shaky hand began, continuing in a tone addressed to Little Rita.

This morning, we were just finishing breakfast when Win paled, put down her spoon and said we had to go to Blaby Copse and see Norrie." You haven't finished your Force Flakes," said Alf, "I've got toast. Plus, the babbie's in a routine, it's hard for Shirl now she's finished work, and I have a man to meet… "

"No." Said Win. "Now."

"Alf's right," I protested, "Rita's not changed, her frock's only just on. She needs her bottle."

"She'll have to feed on the way. We need to go, now, get her shoes, coat, and bonnet."

I remembered a fairy tale we got read at school, frightening me. Someone swapped a good woman's baby for an elf-changeling. A white witch came by the cottage, took one look at the baby, and knew what had happened. She told the woman to break eggs, fill the remains of shell with water, and boil them on the hob. The woman did as she was told. The baby sat-up in the cradle, though it now had the face of an old elf-man. "I have seen the hen before the egg, I have seen the sun before the moon, but never did I see water boiled in egg shells," it shrieked, before flying-off and vanishing up the chimney. Grandwem had the voice of that changeling as she spoke.

"'Later, love, they're busy," put in George.

"Later's too late: now!" She persisted.

George stopped in his tracks,"'What have you seen, Win?"

"It were a feelin' about our Norrie. I'll go me sen."

"No," said Alf, "fair do's – We'll all go."

Grandwem's coat and hat were on before we knew, she'd shovelled the remaining "Force" down, and gone upstairs. She returned with baby-things, and taking you from my knee, started to dress you. A bottle'd been left to cool, so was almost ready. "We've no time" Grandwem said, and I remembered that when I asked our teacher if the woman in the story got her real baby back, she'd said "probably," which did nothing to re-assure.

"Get the pram and your coat, Alfred, there's no work today,' our changeling said.

We knew what Win's visions meant, too well to say no. I recalled her woman in grey, seen or felt trailing her, just before Rita died. It was bang on the money. Then there was her drowned man, Rita's ex-beau, seen returning to those awful buildings he'd grown-up in. Except they weren't there anymore and neither, it seems, was he.

I went for my coat, and the bottle, Alf took you from Win and headed for the Silver Cross pram Court had bought, and George was already dressed when we looked up. On the way, you took your bottle good as gold, as if used to feeding on the hoof. "That's 'cos your lot come from tinkers," Alf laughed. When we settled you back in the pram, sleep soon followed. "Not bad, gyppo with a Silver Cross." I said. George and Grandwem hurried in front as if there was a fire behind.

It took an hour to get to Blaby Copse. "Funny," mused Grandwem, falling back to talk to us, "when I were a lass, most of this were fields. The town's spreading. Blaby Copse is one of't only wild places left. I bet Council'd like to build homes on it." By the time we arrived, air had warmed, and we could see paint peeling from the front of Norrie's caravan.

"This is the first year it's not been titivated since wartime," Grandwem said, "Council's tried to move him, times, but he told 'em if that caravan went, he went wi all his menagerie."

The copse seemed to be breathing in. As well as canines ranged round caravan-wheels, there was a lone hare, standing eyeing us, right before the steps. The hare looked at Win, flecked eyes seeming to hold hers with fellow-feeling. I almost expected it to speak. I swear, it raised itself all its length, until we could see the dandelion-clock belly fur straddled by elastic limbs. It held her gaze, swivelled, and loped off. Eventually, it stood sentinel under a nearby Rowan.

"Tree of the cross. He knows." Grandwem said in a whisper, "Norrie's gone."

"Should've been a single magpie," said George.

"Ah."

Alf and I could've contradicted. Said Norrie lay-in. We knew better.

Shirl thought of the woman in grey, hounding Grandwem before Rita died. Wondering why she hadn't appeared, she'd continued writing:

We parked the pram and Alf took you, humming "Mary from the Dairy" under his breath as we made our way up caravan steps. There'd been a fire nearby, which was stamped out, but still had a toasting fork stuck in. The hare watched our progress from under the Rowan.

Inside, all seemed as it should be. The only sound was from a harlequin-enamel kettle singing on the pot-bellied-stove (whose pipe became the caravan's chimney). Through steam we saw a racing calendar from The Dogs, red-velvet curtains, a table with an Old English Roses tea-cup waiting to be filled, and a plate bearing slices of toast.

Norrie was curled on his settle, plaid blanket over his legs. One of the pups snuggled beside him. It was as if he'd fallen asleep awaiting the kettle's boiling. Underneath his settle, a box of pups squirmed and mewled.

Grandwem went, bending next to him. "There brother, my last brother," she crooned as if singing for them both, "Oh, he's gone, he's gone. Last of all my lot, even his Ada, his own little lass, went before he did."

Gently, she removed the pup, hugging it, and rocking on squashed heels. For it was then I noticed she still had carpet slippers on, and looking down, I realised, so had I.

That was it, really. Nothing to be done. Alf handed you back to me, took the kettle off, adding water to the cup. George went in search of further cups, and tea. "The milk's under the steps," said Grandwem. "It were peaceful," she continued, "Right. We'll take the dogs home wi' us, then come back. We've things to do, but the dogs need attending. He'd've wanted that."

I sniffled into your baby hat. "He's with Mam and Mattie and the rest now, and your sister. Let's get on with rounding-up the dogs," said Grandwem. So we did. Now we're back, waiting to go out again.

Shirl shut the book, snapping the clasp to strains of Alf resuming "Mary from the Dairy" to pacify his daughter.

Trouble with Norrie

Shirl, Alf, Grandwem and George were back in Norrie's caravan. They'd left baby Rita with Mrs Webb, a neighbour who said with nine kids one more made no difference. "And none of mine's babbies no more, Win, and I miss the cuddly little souls," she added.

Shirl couldn't believe how that day's events unfolded: Win's "feeling" over her Force Flakes resulting in that flight to Norrie's; ending with them finding him dead in his beloved caravan. When they returned, Shirl thought it must be a mistake - they'd see him on the steps, greeting them with, "Some silly beggars have been here while I slept, drank all me tea." Then Grandwem and George could go off to their work in the cinema, and she could fetch Rita back. It was a vain hope.

For there he lay, still covered by his old plaid. The hare that'd met them on first arrival, was settled below the steps, moving not an inch when they went in. Everything seemed stilled. Even the birdsong, Shirl thought, appeared to have lessened, as if they bloody knew.

Shirl always considered Norrie a man of few possessions. Yet looking around she realised space was crammed, cigar boxes and fruit-crates bulging. This trip, Alf had retrieved

109

the car from Swain's Garage where it had been to have a new tyre fitted, so they could bring stuff back. A lopsided bookshelf was full of titles such as *The Home Medical Enquirer,* and *The Dog Fancier's Daily Round.*

Alf broke silence.

"Well," he said, "I'm stretching me legs, and going to that phone box on *Sprockett's Way,* we need the quack to tell us what's what, then the undertakers… then I have to phone that fancy hotel our Billy's holed-up in."

"No Alfred, not yet. We have to seek-out his last wishes first." Said Grandwem.

"But he'll need to be taken, love."

"Yes, but taken right. When *we* know what's what."

"Did he have a solicitor, Win?"

"One used to come. They disagreed, the man wouldn't always do as Norrie wanted."

Grandwem paused as if she was going to say something else, an ominous sign, Shirl knew.

"I'll look in that big box near the stove, said he allus kept important doings in there," said Grandwem. The large crate stamped *Spratt's Wormer* looked an unlikely treasure chest, but inside were a large morocco-leather picture album, a book of postcards, a letter addressed "To Winifred Bean," and a substantial envelope marked "My Will."

Grandwem passed the letter to Alf, commanding, Read it out."

"Dere Win", he began, "if you are reading this, I am gone. Do not grieve, I was happy and had a good innings. I'm now with me daughter and brothers and Mam, and all, so be it. My will is here, but the solicitor, Mr Dove, got stroppy at it, and said he would not oversee such eccentric

110

wishes. You will see why. Please try and carry them out – you need to contact Gypsy Sayers for help, though he often turns up at such times. If he still lives, that is, him being older than we. He agreed to the deed long since. Sorry to saddle you with dogs, Peggy, my owl, and hare. The hare will go with Sayers if he comes. If you call with the whistle near the door, Peggy will take your arm, and come home with you. Blessings to all, Norrie."

"What deed?" said Alf, "And an owl to take home, me car'll be splattered."

By this time, Grandwem had opened her brother's will, and was reading it shaking her head, and sucking at her teeth so hard gums rasped.

"He allus said it as a joke, I thought. Niver reckoned he meant it."

"Meant what?" asked George.

"He wants a bleddy Viking funeral. Wants to be burned up, along with his caravan."

"No wonder the solicitor quailed," Alf laughed, "Well, we can't do that, Win. Last wishes or not, you can't just go setting fires. I'm not a fan of the right side of the law, but I would be over that. You could burn the Copse down!"

"That fire's what Gypsy Sayers's for. He's done it before now."

"Look, Ma," said Shirl. "We need a death certificate. I know Norrie didn't have many papers, but even he had to get coupons during the war."

"He shared, we divvied up for him."

"Ma! The authorities'd have us. We'd be up in court and like as not in stir, and me and Alf just parents. They'd take Rita off us. I'm sorry, I loved Uncle Norrie much as anyone, but this is the 1960s, not the dark ages, with gypsies and burnings. Burnt with his caravan – like... like... *The Beverly Hillbillies.*"

"More like *The Ashfield In-Breeders*," chortled Alf, "and I don't think even the Clampitts would burn Grandma. Look, Win, I can't become a jail-bird when my girls need me."

"Well Alfred," said Grandwem, "You've had your say, and I reckon you're right, though it sticks in my craw not to do what he wanted. Now, go to that phone box and call the doctor, then the undertakers – Speed's not Brown and Wasson, we don't want to end-up wi' a hardboard coffin like something from *Hobbies for Boys!*"

Alf returned, saying Doctor Wragg was on his way (having said he'd contact the undertakers who'd have to take Norrie to the hospital - as he'd died on his tod, there'd be enquiries). Billy was out, but a message had been left with the hotel.

They sat and made tea, while occasionally someone took a desultory look at Norrie's things. Doctor Wragg came and, having seen, covered Norrie with a white sheet, and said the undertakers were due to take him at five. "There was an owl in one of the trees," he said, "and a hare sitting under here." He told them he was pretty sure Norrie died of natural causes, but you never knew. Then, Wragg left, saying he too would be back at five.

"I could have told him natural causes." Grandwem sighed. "Hospital'll cut me brother up, he'd have hated that."

"I'm sorry," Shirl sobbed, taking her hand.

"He were always a daft beggar," said Grandwem, "get me that album from the box."

They opened the album lifted from the *Spratt's Wormer* treasure-chest. The first picture showed a baby in a monster perambulator. The baby sported a big frilly hat, long skirts, and a cardboard moustache. "Me Mam put it on him for a giggle, and he were daft ever since!" said Grandwem.

The following picture revealed a good looking young man, with real waxed moustache. He was clad in long white footballer's shorts, thin black socks, and a striped shirt. By his side was an identically dressed Jack Russell standing on its hind-legs, sans moustache. "That were Norrie's first dancing dog, taken at Lammas Fair."

Knocking disturbed Grandwem's reverie. Shirl opened-up to reveal a weasel-thin individual, skin the colour of beech leaves. Oiled coat reached round his ankles, and a large inky hat offset white curls and glimmering ear-ring. He spoke to her through gilded teeth.

"Missus, I'm Gypsy Sayers. I was wanted, for the rai within." He said.

"Rye?" Shirl whispered.

"Rai. It means 'gentleman'," said Grandwem, "tell him he's welcome."

Two nights later saw Shirl once more writing in her converted diary:

Well, Rita. Sometimes, things sort themselves, no matter what's planned. Grandwem dismissed Gypsy Sayers, after we'd had tea with him. Before leaving, he said he'd make sure and visit us as he'd things to tell. He also informed there'd been thefts in the area, and to be sure and take Norrie's things home with us in the car. "An empty caravan's a gift to those headed for staripen," he said. I think he meant prison.

Last we saw of him, was him and the hare loping off, late sun on their backs.

At five, Doctor Wragg returned, telling us the undertakers were delayed, and wouldn't be there until seven. We decided to take Gypsy Sayers' advice, and load Alf's car up, going home 'till later. I was keen to get you back from Mrs Webb.

Oh yes, and Peggy, the owl, came. Alf blew the whistle when we were outside, and she arrived, fixing on Grandwem's arm. She was no trouble in the car, and now sits on the roof of the outdoor lavvy, like she did when waiting for Norrie.

So. we got home, un-loaded some of Norrie's things, and went inside. Grandwem looked dog-tired, but perked up singing and clapping to you. Alf and I said we'd leave you, her and George at home, and go back to the caravan and wait. We decided to walk, as there was still stuff in the car.

At about ten to seven, we were still a way from Blaby Copse when we saw it, a plume of smoke lit red from below. Air was acrid. As we got nearer, heat rose, and we knew the caravan to be blazing.

Months later, Shirl made an addition to this entry, in different coloured ink:

When Police made their enquiries, and investigated, they came to the conclusion the caravan had been struck by freak lightning. It would have to be "freak" as we had no storm that night. Undertakers had been delayed by other calls, but wouldn't even have got there at seven, being held-up again by a fallen tree and, later, by a man who'd appeared out of nowhere on the road, making them stall and break down. So the doctor told us.

A good while after this entry, Shirl added further post-script:

Two funny things concerning Norrie. Though Grandwem, as per usual, took these in her stride, saying they were "fitting."

First, though we were sure Gypsy Sayers had hand in setting the fire, Police remained content with their "lightning" theory. Alf expected them to come round saying they'd revised their ideas. They never did.

But the second's even odder. A few weeks ago, Grandwem got a letter from Wren Ragley, one of Norrie's old drinking pals, who'd read of the fire in the local paper. He doesn't live round here, so his sister sends the Chad on.

"Well, Win," he wrote, "that's another 'ewd un' gone to his maker. My brother's dead too, Maxie, recall Maxie? Lad who got his head stuck in the school railings? By coincidence, I came across an obituary for old Gypsy Sayers, recently, remember him? Norrie, he, and I had high times when we joined him on the road when we were nowt but youths. He was our senior. He had a tame hare, remember?"

The man sent a cutting, some of which is pasted here –
GYPSY SAYERS – KING OF THE HIGH ROADS
DIES ON WAY TO APPLEBY HORSE FAIR

This has a big description of his funeral which was dated a good month before we found Norrie. "Maybe we saw his son." I said to Grandwem, but she just smiled.

This account says among the tributes was a floral sculpture in the shape of a leaping hare.

"Well, I call that champion," said Grandwem when we first read it. "You know, in our day, mates always made a big point of coming home to help each other out in times of need." And she left me pondering, as she went to feed Peggy a dead mouse from the trap.

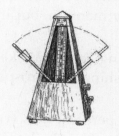

The Snare

I.

"Well, all's I know is, we can't have a normal funeral." Grandwem had pontificated weeks after the fire at Norrie's caravan. "As there's precious little left to bury. I've talked to t' Vicar about a stone, and he weren't keen at first. Said I wanted the stone there before us, I've sorted that wi' a stonemason, Reg Cant (he's nearly as ewd as Norrie, and knew him). He'll do it champion. The Vicar weren't keen on Norrie or the early stone, or Reg, thought they were all heathen. But I reminded him as his predecessor, who worshipped the ales as much as owt, were a bit of an heathen, too."

"So the Police are happy for us to have a funeral?"

"Ah. I don't think we'll be troubled more, George."

Grandwem sucked in her teeth. "A quick burial, I'll read summat appropriate, then the Vicar'll say the necessary. Then a Wake, up at that pub near Blaby Copse."

"What," said Alf, "The Snare? Rough as a badger's arse. Good job we'll probably have a police escort."

"That's as may be. But it's nearest to where Norrie lived, and the landlady says Shirl and I can go and clean before the

117

day. I know it's all nowt nor summat, and the Wake's in a pub we'd not normally mention, but it's the best I can come up wi' to suit Norrie."

"Well, who's coming to the Wake, besides us?' asked Shirl, already not relishing the prospect of cleaning a flea-bitten pub.

"Now that's a reet perplexer, as you'd be surprised how many folk Norrie knew. There's the Doctor, Courtney, Billy, Mighty Rosco, Ernie Fields, he met Norrie through Court. Then there's that ewd lass as scratches her sen against posts and trees. And what about your lot, Alfred?"

"Sid's not well, and Bee's looking after him."

"You know you mentioned that old woman who scratches on posts", Shirl put in sniffily, "do you mean that person they call Dirty Ida in town?"

"That's her."

"Lovely," said Shirl, "a filthy pub and filthy guests."

"Now, she wasn't always as she is now. Believe it or not, she was a pretty young woman, worked for the ice cream man, did bike deliveries. She and Norrie once had a fling. No, Ida weren't always ragged, you lot tek folk at face value. It's a funeral, she'll come clean for it."

"Blimey! Now that I'd pay to see," said Alf, "Still I bet the authorities'll be glad to be shut of us. I've seen their faces 'burnt in his caravan, they're all tinkers', that's what they've been thinkin' down the Cop Shop."

"So," interrupted George, "are we puttin' the date in the *Chad*? If it's not in the paper, people miss it."

"Already done. I've given us till two weeks on Thursday."

II.

Shirl thought about shows Beryl was designing for – with snappy titles like *Summertime Parade* and *Beat on Sea*. These blended variety with more modern acts, and Beryl was designing sparkly short dresses and flaring suits in acid pinks and blues. People twisted, had hair big as busbies, sprayed sticky, and mini-skirts shining like light bulbs. These candy-floss palettes seemed worlds away from the jet frock Grandwem had worn since Norrie went.

They'd left upstairs curtains closed, covered mirrors with nut-brown velvet cloths produced from the cellar, and Alf had been made to go down Willow Avenue and tell old Mrs Down's bees Norrie was no more.

"I felt a right 'nana, leaning down to a hive and saying: 'Norrie's dead."

"Well, these things have to be done right," said Grandwem, "or he'll not rest."

"I can smell his pipe, in the outside lavvy," said Shirl, "and hear his paper rustling."

"Well, Love, he was here a long time; folk don't just go, you know."

People started calling in with their respects, elderly individuals Shirl hadn't encountered before. They chucked Little Rita under the chin, pinched her cheek, and went to talk to the owl, who usually sat on the bench by the back door. She and Alf were surprised by the sheer number of callers...

People whose dogs Norrie had wormed or rescued ...'my terrier, Jap, got kicked by an horse, and left for dead. Your Norrie put a poultice on him, smelt fierce as *Swarfega*, and the dog got up after a few minutes, good as new'...

119

'Rameses, me little pug, were right chill, we thought him near the brink. Old Norrie brought him back. This here's Rameses III, and we've brought you one of his pups for comfort. Maybe your babby would like to have him?'

Thus far, they'd two new pups, one tame hedgehog, and a sour-faced kitten to find room for. But it wasn't the gifted animals that got to Shirl but people arriving with tales of kindnesses his family had known nothing of. A starved looking girl with straggly blonde plaits, who Grandwem immediately started to feed up with seed cake, told how, for two years or more, Norrie paid her bus fare to her Mother's.

"I got the bus and hoped the Conductress wouldn't come until I was off. Norrie was in the seat in front of me, and when the woman asked for the fare, I cried and said I hadn't got it. She was all for throwing me off, but he paid. Waited for me in the same spot each week and gave me my fare. I said, one day, I'd pay him back, but he said he didn't want it, that I was his good deed for the week. Funny, but last time I saw him, he gave me a note and said that should be a good few fares to come, as if he knew. I still have the note, do you want it back, Mrs Bean?"

"I reckon its yours, and, when it runs out, you knock on my door. Now, I'll put some of that cake in a bag for you."

Then there was a woman who said he'd looked out old clothes for her. "They were from a trunk, I think they'd belonged to his other brothers, but they fit my Arthur lovely. A bit old fashioned I suppose, but no one said anything at the factory."

The tale bringing a lump to Shirl's throat was from a man sporting a spectacular black eye. He'd stood at the back door, wringing his cap like someone from an old film, but wouldn't come in. "I'll not stay. I just wanted to say your brother was a jewel to me, one in thousands... You see, our Belle, my Missus, well... she's a violent temper on her when she gets one on. Your Norrie used to give us sanctuary, me and the boy. Her rages never last. It's when she's been out. She don't mean it, I swear. I never told no one. Your brother found me down the lane, one time she'd hit me wi' a bottle. He took me to his caravan, cleaned me up and put something on the cuts. It were for terriers, but it healed me lovely. It don't seem much, but he told me I could come any time. I think he saved me boy. I sent him to Norrie when she got proper bad. I'll go now. Thanks for hearing. Don't say owt."

Shirl told him he and the boy could come to her, or Grandwem, anytime.

"The Boy's sent off." He said. "He's joined the Navy, now. It seemed for the best."

All of the visitors said they wouldn't miss the Wake, graveside being family only. "Bloody hell," said Alf, "we'll need to knock-through in that pub, their best room's really titchy."

III.

The day before Norrie's funeral, Shirl and Grandwem took a crate of bleach, Tide, Windolene, Dettol, and other products to The Snare. Carrying the crate from his car, Alf noted windows webbed by generations of spiders - as he got in the car to go back, he thought Grandwem and Shirl had their work cut out for them. Grandwem considered the best room smelt like, and had the appearance of, the inside of a rabbit hutch. Not *her* rabbit hutch, she thought, which was cleaner by a mile. Beer was poured through taps dark and crusted as old sausages.

"I done me best, but since me man went, I never was one for cloths and water," said Mrs Brierly, the landlady, "you just do it, then it has to be done again."

Privately, both Shirl and Grandwem thought she'd never done it, as the whole place was furred with neglect. A good day's work, though, and the place shone like George's teeth after a night in the glass.

"Well, I never," said Mrs Brierly. "you've done it all, and fair put me to shame. Tomorrow, I'll put me clean frock on, and those stockings I squirreled away at Christmas. I won't let you down, Mrs Bean."

"Thank you. We can't have a lying in tonight, as there's no full body, but, if it's all the same to you, we might come and put some pictures on the wall and light a candle."

"That's fine. I'll have some fruit wine put by, same as for the day itself. It's greengage, and I have plum and Sloe-gin. My man was a marvel at the fruit wines, taught me well before he went."

IV.

Mrs Brierly's greengage wine was gold as honey, making you smell summer orchards. She'd found boxes of multi-coloured glasses in the cellar, washed them, so liquid glinted through ruby, emerald, and cobalt. "We got these on promotion before the war, but the place never looked good enough to put them out," she said.

Pictures of Norrie (baby with a moustache, young man accompanied by dancing dog) graced the wall where a five years out of date calendar and a chipped mirror had once hung. "When my man died," said Mrs Brierly, "I realise that I carried on but didn't. Your spring clean meant the world

122

to me, even if it was for a sad reason. I'll continue the good works, seeing it all gleamy in this light's grand."

"I forgot to ask," said Grandwem, smiling appreciatively at her green wine glass,"'tomorrow, if it's all the same with you, can we bring animals?"

V.

An owl.

A caged budgie ('George Formby would want to say goodbye' said Grandwem).

Assorted dogs and pups (a few 'bloody gumps' amongst them).

One hedgehog.

A grumpy-looking kitten that had nipped everyone on the way there in the car and, outside, so someone said, a hare.

Not the usual Wake, the doctor thought. But Mrs Brierly's fruit wines gave you summer hedges, fields at dusk, and paths lost since childhood. The graveside gathering of a few family, police officer, and doctor, had been quiet, and black as crows. Before the vicar did the usual, Grandwem had read:

"Now the joys of the road are chiefly these:

A crimson touch on the hard-wood trees;

A vagrant's morning wide and blue

In the early fall, when the wind walks, too."

"Now that's Bliss Carman," the vicar mouthed to the doctor. "Canadian. Not so heathen as you'd think."

The stone had been a marvel. A white erect slab, carved with the image of an owl and caravan, and bearing one word, "Norrie." No surname, date or phrase, and near the older part of the cemetery, rather than close to a lot of newer graves. "Us Mam and Dad's nearby." Grandwem explained. "He'd like that." The Vicar had hoped it was far enough from where a visiting Bishop might walk for them to get away with a pagan slab with no dates. Still, at least the family had worn black, that was something. As they'd quit the graveside for cars waiting to take them to The Snare, a far off transistor could be heard playing The Beatles - *I'll Follow the Sun.* It somehow seemed appropriate.

VI.

A crowd pushed around *The Snare* as the family arrived. All, young or old, clutching wild flowers – ragged robin, dog roses, meadowsweet. It reminded Alf of the school nature table and the push to place the best bird's egg there. The crowd parted as extended family walked in: Grandwem and George; Alf, Shirl, Beryl, and Little Rita; Billy, Courtney and Ernie Fields; the Mighty Rosco with Peggy, the owl, on his arm. All following, for pork pie, crisps, sandwiches, coronation chicken and, Norrie's favourite, pork scratchings.

Soon, fruit wine flowed and tales began... the time Norrie rode his penny-farthing through someone's house when front and back door were open ... the wriggling bag he pulled from Nottingham's canal that turned-out to have the Lord Lieutenant's dog in it... the girls he'd almost married before producing Ada, and the great escapes he'd had until the last ...

Someone sang, as it grew dusk, favourites from long ago: *There's an Old Mill by the Stream, Nellie Dean*, delivered by a beautiful old woman in a twilight coloured dress, with a blue crystal necklace at her throat. "What a lovely voice." Said Shirl.

"Aye. Ida used to sing at the cinema, between reels."

"What, that's Dirty Ida?"

"Yes,' said Grandwem, 'Told you she'd clean up lovely.'

"I used to call for him with my sister, take him to the boxing," one old girl reminisced, "we thought he'd tek a shine to one on us, but he never did."

VII.

Ernie Fields had never seen such a big funeral. Increasingly, during the tea, his eyes turned to Beryl. They'd met before, but there was something different about her now, a grown look about the set of her mouth and eyes. He loved the passionate way she talked about work, and the softness with which she seemed to regard her little niece. She chatted to some visiting gypsies, all done out in purples and mulberries, their hats stuck with raven plumes. "I'd love to draw you, in case I ever need a costume like yours," she was saying. Then one of the women took her hand, and said something, at which Beryl made her excuses and went outside.

Ernie followed. "Did she say something to upset you?" He asked.

"No," she said, pushing a stray hair back into her beehive. "No. She just said how they loved Norrie, and I miss him. Thanks for asking."

Beryl felt the woman's words ("That little lass of yourn is in the best place. You should never take her from it by thought or deed") must be etched on her eyes. But Ernie smiled; she'd not given herself away.

"It does you credit, Beryl, feeling things so much." He said. Beryl liked his sad smile.

"Look, I don't suppose this is the right time, but I'm going back with Courtney tonight, and I'm playing a special at The Royal tomorrow lunchtime. It's a benefit. I'm free in the evening, though, I don't suppose you'd fancy meeting for a meal at the Flying Horse? Might do you good."

Even as Beryl heard herself saying "Yes" she was filled with the thought, after all that had gone on with Little Rita, she deserved a lot less than the glad eye from Ernie Fields.

Dominoes

"We look like old pub regulars watching the girls."

"And not in a good way."

Billy and Court were confronting *Pop It*, seated next to Grandwem Win and George. George's mouth was too crammed with Nestle's to proffer opinion, as was Alf's, who was standing behind the settee. But Grandwem, bouncing Little Rita on her knee, in time to Big Webbly, was rapt.

"Look at that girl's skirt, you can nigh-on see her bottom!"

"She hasn't got much bottom to regard." Alf managed to splutter. "Nowt to hold on to in the dark."

"Alfred!"

"It's true," laughed George, unwrapping more chocolate, "like a cherry on a stick wi' out the cherry. Now, in our day, girls was girls. She's got hair like a little lad."

"Eton Crop, they called it, years back. Some had it at the factory."

"Well thank the Lord not the ones I fancied, Win. A right shame."

"I like it," Shirl came in, her arms full of washing. "That one there's a bit like Twiggy, grand."

127

"She is that." Grandwem agreed, "but she'd be even grander with a couple of offal pies inside her."

Court went to the kitchen to fetch a brown ale. When he came back, George was still on about Twiggy and her boyish hair. "Now Win still has lovely hair, and to say we're gettin' on, it's still brown as a nut. Show 'em Win, tek yer turban off."

"Oh, they don't want to see my old locks."

'We do, show your Great Granddaughter.' Shirl said.

So Grandwem obliged, carefully unpinning the roller at her hair's front, and removing the turban, which was seemingly constructed of several pieces of grey fabric.

Underneath, hair was tightly pinned into little curls that clung to her scalp. The hair looked thin, and Shirl doubted George's description it could still be brown. Pin after pin cascaded onto the kidney-table near the telly, chink, chink, chink.

"Blimey," Court whistled, "now that's what I call something."

Unpinned, Grandwem's hair reached below her knees and was waved chestnut brown, flecked with grey. It was the loveliest hair, Court thought, he'd ever seen, even on showgirls. Remembering Rita's hair, of a similar thickness and wave to Grandwem's, Shirl sniffed.

"That's enough of that dog-and-monkey show," Grandwem snorted, retrieving the pins and re-placing them, turban, and roller with such alacrity Billy thought she'd've made a mean novelty act. "I was thinking of our Rita," said Shirl, "she'd beautiful curls, like yours... here's hoping the little one gets them."

Court thought of the Twiggy girls, their Italian suited male counterparts, next to these he and Billy looked like old men. How could their TV careers survive what the papers were calling a "youth quake?"

Then there was that incident with Mr Gin at the recording. They'd not heard from him since, at least that was something. Yet, Court was almost ashamed at what had gone on. The man was bad and desperate. Even if, as an act, he was also desperately bad.

"Ere, you're missing yus sens, you're back on." Grandwem called to Court, who was back in the kitchen seeking a home-made pork pie from the pantry.

"Two old boys at a swinging club, Win? I can do without it, and so can your Bill."

"Now, now. Still - as you're in that mood, bring me and George a pie n'all, I can hear you rustling."

Billy had to admit extracts from the *New Beat* tour looked slick and more televisual than old variety turns sometimes hosted on their show. They'd have to invite more modern guests if they wanted to stay on top, and learn some new songs. If Billy had but known it, his partner was thinking along similar lines, as he balanced three pork pies on one plate.

The baby, now being jiggled along to Little Carmen, was laughing. Her little face was joyous, and the belly laugh infectious. "I want to hold you... want to love you/ that's why I scold you/that's why I hurt you, too."

"Well, at least somebody's happy," said Billy, clapping in Little Rita's direction.

"And so should you be," Grandwem said, "you've got your face on a plastic television, folk recognise you in the streets, and you've got more brass than a mucky swank on

Derby Day. Yet here are you and Courtney, mithering if it'll last. Sometimes, I think you want too much. Do wages last? No, folk earn 'em all week and they go down the throat of a Saturday night. Do looks last if you have any? One day you stare in the mirror and your face's tight as skin on a rice pudding, the next it looks like what's under the bleddy surface. Did our Rita's time last? We all know the answer to that one. Enjoy it lads, enjoy it as it goes, that's all I'm saying."

"She's right," said Alf, "I look in the mirror when I'm dolled-up, and see Clark Gable, but under me shirt and kecks it's a different matter."

"When I were twenty,' said George, 'I had a tattoo done on me arm that were meant to be a bluebird. Now it looks like a bleddy vulture."

"I know we're ungrateful sods," Court said, "but I think we have to face the music and embrace changes if we want to stay on top. What say you, Billy boy?"

"Think you're right. We should have more acts like those *New Beat*-ers, if we want to keep the young ones watching. I mean, look, even the baby likes them."

"That's the boys,' said Grandwem, 'but just you remember us oldies'll be tuning in, too. If there's nowt for us, we'll hit the switch and it'll be dominoes. Speaking of which, take the Babby, Shirl, I'll go and fetch ours."

Click.

Determination on Grandwem and Courtney's faces.

Click.

An expanding pattern of liquorice coloured slabs with ivory dots.

Click.

Grandwem always beat anyone who played her.

Click. Click.

"Bugger!" Courtney's concentration let him down.

Click. Sup.

Grandwem knew she was the victor.

CLICK.

"George, it's your turn, Mr Cooper's finished. I done for him like Viking hordes swarming over a farm in a Kirk Douglas film."

Between games, small hands reached for dominoes, occasionally winning and pushing them to the floor. Sometimes, a pup or kitten would wreak havoc with the table.

"We'll consult management, Bill." Court said.

"Yes."

"That's settled, then."

"Do that, boys," said Grandwem, "but in the meantime, enjoy yus sens."

In the background, George Formby struck-up with a few bars of *Mr Wu*, followed by Little Carmen's *I Want to Love You* – song he'd newly cottoned onto from the television.

Picnic

Grandwem received a letter from Beryl, telling her she was walking out with Ernie Fields:

Of course, Beryl wrote, *I won't tell him of recent events, which goes hard with me, as I don't relish secrets kept. They only lead to trouble, in my book. Still, the situation's my own fault, I suppose you'd say, if I hadn't been so daft none of this would've happened.*

"Aye,' sighed Grandwem, 'and Shirl wouldn't be half as content, and she and Alf wouldn't be bothered with their lovely little lass."

Well, continued the letter, *as you know, Ernie's more than I deserve, and, really, I should tell him before things get serious. But I won't, and he'll just have to put up with someone who doesn't tell him everything. I'll bet he can see it in my face. But I shan't say and that's that.*

Grandwem hoped that *was* well and truly that. There'd been enough heartache. She thought of Norrie, dead and gone. Somehow her brother's passing seemed to underline bigger changes afoot. As expected, the Council seized on the idea of Blaby Copse soon as the caravan was burnt, and what was left of her Brother buried. As far as they could ascertain, Norrie hadn't owned the land on which he'd lived for decades.

Mr Simpkin, hosiery factory owner, had rights to Blaby Copse, and'd always had a soft spot for Norrie, once telling

Grandwem, "It's nice to see some bogger who don't live by rules that some of the rest of us shackle us sens wi."

Now, the Council was all over Simpkin to sell Norrie's spot and the Copse with it, to be built on. Grandwem knew it was only a matter of time, before her Brother's beloved place of habitation became a square of small, neat houses.

'And why not?' She asked herself. 'There's plenty of folk live in squalor as'd kill for a nice house, somewhere wi' trees.' Yet in her heart of hearts, Grandwem felt it wasn't the folk living in squalor that would be moved into Blaby Copse. Her persistent vision increasingly became one of a posh square with a few elms and beeches left for effect, and a copse that was prime for other developments – giving up its magpies, dead-man's-ear fungus, and harebells for signs reading *Copse Heights – Be Part of It*. As matter-of-course, she thought, there would be room for several motor cars.

She saw shiny magazine headlines in the Dentist's waiting room:

MANSFIELD TO BECOME BOOM TOWN

and

WE'RE ON THE WAY UP.

Those pieces were accompanied by photos of her Billy (LOCAL LAD NOW TV STAR) various businessmen leaning over documents or signing contracts with fixed smiles and, once, their Beryl: OUR MISS POTTER, COSTUMIER TO THE STARS.

"So that's it, the Beans and Potters, putting Mansfield on the map," she'd said aloud. "We'll be mucky swanks next, swanning it at The Savoy in Nottingham, noses aloft."

Still, Mansfield's shops *were* looking smart, like the newly done-up Swales' Grocers, also in the papers, shiny counters

134

defined by the phrase FAMILY GROCERS TO NEW SUPERMARKET – WHAT MANSFIELD'S FUTURE LOOKS LIKE.

Grandwem went to the store's opening with the rest of the town, but she missed "silly things, really": the vacuum tube propelling orders and money to the elevated central payment desk, where plump Old Mrs Swales used to sit in state; pats of butter cut and wrapped in greaseproof; the huge wheel of the bacon-slicer with its squeaky hum, the same slicer that had shivered its way through meat since Grandwem's childhood.

"Everything's gorra sign, 'this off' and 'that bargain,'" said Mrs Hills, pulling at her new stockings at the opening. "Looks cheaper to me."

"It should be bleddy cheaper, we've spent enough on it," replied young Mr Swales who'd overheard. "Cheaper's what's wanted these days, that and pre-packed. It's enabled us to get rid of the old slicer, and having to measure the tea out by hand. We have leaf-tea (boxed), and bags, so the old barrels and brass scoops went to the bin-men. Me Dad were upset when the slicer went, it had been his Dad's. Still, 'honest Jo', it were only a matter of time before it stuck and had a finger. Made more noise than Dad's false teeth."

In fact, Grandwem had *had* to attend Swales' opening, as Courtney and Billy cut the ribbon.

Grandwem had worn her Saturday hat, squashed felt decorated with a pheasant feather pin found at Norrie's, and a new mustard coloured coat. The whole family had been in attendance. "Don't smell of anything," Billy noted, "that's my abiding memory of Swales' – tangy tea, what was that exotic one you loved, Ma? They got down to the last grains of it during the war."

"Cherry Leaf."

'That's it, got it in one, Cherry Leaf. Smelled of rich floor wax, and may blossoms. Then there was that meaty pong near the back, and, remember that year the butter heated up?"

"Like custard made wi' dried milk-powder, ran summat horrible," laughed Grandwem.

"Pilchards," Court'd joined in, "Billy used to bring those tinned pilchards, but the paper bag smelled of that tea you mentioned, Win."

New Swales' had odour of Zoflora and Dettol, and was white as a fresh toilet bowl. Gone, mahogany with brass fixings, those mysterious drawers with names picked-out in gilt. Vanished, the cobalt and cream butchery aisle, with plaster pig, all striped apron, cleaver, and wink. And missing were the vast tea barrels decorated with Chinese maiden transfers in cinnabar red. A lavatory-shiny world now, tiles, plastic, formica, and melamine, to which Mrs Hills responded: "Oh look, Win, they've had them marmite surfaces put in!" Old Mr Swales, shaking Billy's hand for a photograph, looked disconsolate.

First Swales' then, a few months after Norrie's burial, Grandwem was proved right, and the Copse was to go. Simpkin gave in, a notice being nailed to an oak of planning consent to erect a set of houses. There was wording to effect that a sense of place would be maintained, and not all trees felled, but no one who'd seen similar sites was convinced.

"One day, soon," Grandwem said to Shirl, "we'll tek our Little Rita back to see it as it was when Norrie loved it. We'll have a picnic, even if it's perishing, and drink to him. Then I'll not walk there more. I've no desire to see it gone."

Shirl knew better than argue, writing to Beryl:

So, Norrie's Copse is to go, old Simpkin sold-up - not that I bad-mouth him like some folk are doing. But Win's taken it hard. The last of her brothers, his caravan burnt to ashes, and now the very spot it stood on to be houses. The little beck may be left they say, and a few trees, but it won't be the same, and she doesn't want to see it all built over. I can't say I blame her.

We are to have a picnic soon, so I hope the winds die down!

Our little one continues well, and brings everyone joy. Especially Grandwem and George. You should be proud. I know we're all proud of your job, fancy being in all those posh magazines holding up your designs!

Anyway, back to the Copse - there's to be ten houses initially, small but posh, and it'll be called Copse Way. It's not the only bit of land being built-on, either. Drover's Path's gone, and they're building some shops, including a rival for Swales', where it was. Fancy, Mr Swales spent all that money and now he'll have to compete with a Fine Foods. Oh, yes, and Hosiery Street's having a right face-lift, but they've moved the old residents out to a big Estate near Hucknall, and they're doing the houses up for young families whose dads work at that new cut-price pop factory. I think that Estate's made from the old pre-fabs that they've re-surfaced, wonderful what a bit of asbestos-sheeting can do, Alf says.

At least, I think that's right. I can't keep pace with all the changes. Anyway, back to the Copse. Grandwem says Norrie would have hated to see it built over, but that it's a sign of the times. So, we'll have our picnic, and raise a glass to him, and bugger progress.

As long as they lived, Shirl and Alf wouldn't forget that picnic. It was still windy, but not blowing a gale. Grandwem brought the owl, and George Formby, planting the cage nearby, and letting the owl alight on the car roof. Alf sat on a bacon flan, and the baby laughed herself sick at the sight of him wiping soggy pastry off his trousers. A sound of infant hilarity which George Formby mimicked. "It were worth sitting on it to hear the little 'un laugh like that," said Alf.

Grandwem chortled, too, but her face clouded as they sat, trying to place the caravan's spot, thinking they were seated on it, but then feeling none too certain.

"Oh, well," she said at last,"'it's to go, and that's it. No use mekin' owt out of nowt. Houses are all right, and good luck to them as lives here. At least the spot's pleasant."

"Yeah," Alf said, "apart from that."

He gestured to something vaguely sticky, staked into the ground. "What the bleddy hell is it? Looks like *Hammer Horror*."

"It's an hedgehog skin, 'hotchi-witchi' gypsies call it. They've been here. Paid respects to summat about to go, and feasted on hedge-pig. That bost pin-cushion job's what's left." Said Grandwem, matter-of-factly.

"Urrgh! Eating hedgehog. I call that disgusting, some traditions we're best-off doing without." Shirl was appalled. "They won't be flogging that at Swales'."

"They might," Alf gurgled, "it's cheap. They'd call it something else though: Pickled Prickle, how's that? Still, I bet it tastes like chicken, everything bloody does. Remember that 'mock-chicken' do-dad in the war, Win?"

Grandwem nodded.

"Well that were an irony, the only thing not to taste of chicken."

"I'm not surprised, ours were swede."

Grandwem dug in her string bag, bringing forth three small red plastic cups and a bottle of Mrs Brierly's greengage wine.

"Let's sup to me Brother, who's dead and gone, drink to the Copse and what's past, and then we'll wend us way.' She said. 'Just like the gypsies."

"So long as we don't have to scoff Prickle Pickle", Alf took the bottle, carefully pouring three measures.

Shirl put Little Rita back in her push-chair, covering her legs with a pink crocheted blanket.

"A shame George couldn't be here, but the kinema needed a stock-take," said Grandwem. "I know he'd echo me when I said here's to Norrie, the caravan, and the Copse. Now, look on that hedge-pig skin, you two, and tell Little Rita of it when she grows. Because, chances are, she'll not recall this, and, more than likely, as with me and the gypsies, none of us will walk this way very much again."

"And if we do,' put in Shirl, 'it'll be Copse Way, with shiny front doors and room for parking, and… "

"And," Alf finished for her, "a bleddy over-sized plaster hedgehog, looking down the drive. You could place a bet on it, and win more than your money back."

Those Songs That Break Your Heart

Cooper and Bean had opened a supermarket in Billy's home town, a town that had featured in *Look at Life* as somewhere on the up – "Look at places like Mansfield," the plummy voice-over said, speaking as film of the High Street rolled, "they're on the up and going places. Gone are the old songs whistled by customers in the grocery store" (at this point there was film of young Mr Swales welcoming customers through his shiny white doors) "now it's the piped music of popular hits all the way."

Grandwem and George attended a special preview of *Look at Life* at the cinema where they worked, after closing. "Blimey," said Jago Birch, cinema owner, "you wouldn't recognise us, Win. *I* don't recognise us."

"Cooper and Bean," said the plummy tone, "one of them a local lad done good, now showing on a television set near you."

The film was done after Swales' opening and showed Billy and Court signing photo after photo. In reality, for their fan-club, there was a machine that signed the pictures, which Court hated but recognised a necessary evil. "It don't seem right, the fans want us, and they're our bread-and-butter. They go, we've had it. I know there's too many

141

letters for us to sign every picture, but let's sign as many as we can ourselves, Bill."

Recently, they'd cut a lot of ribbons at shops like *Swales'*, and honoured Court's promise to sign pictures by hand. Billy seemed to enjoy the openings, he was still a looker with his wavy hair and dark eyes, and got a lot of female attention. But Court wondered if there were too many ribbons and not enough soft-shoe.

Maybe this was how life would fold out now – and in Court's notebook came the entry that seemed to define it:

Panto.

TV filming.

Openings etc.

Summer show.

Publicity tour.

TV filming.

Openings etc.

Publicity

Panto.

"Like a hamster on a flaming wheel!" He breathed. On their last phone call to Grandwem, her using the phone they'd had installed in her house, which she bellowed down as if everyone was deaf, she'd shouted that "OLD MESTER SWALES DIED, COLLAPSED OUTSIDE THAT NEW SHOP. I THINK THEY BROKE HIS HEART."

Court thought so, too. "Poor old bugger," said Billy, "I phoned the son to say how sorry we were, and he was beside himself. Said his Dad missed the tea, and the slicer, and hated that piped music they had put in."

"He thought he was doing the right thing, management wise, that lad," said Court, "Now he'll have to compete with bloody Fine Foods, but he wasn't to know that, eh?"

And them, what were they competing with? With *Summer-Ride Special*, *The New Comics*, and *Opportunity Knocks* – so they'd been told at the Studio.

Life was now so different from the zig-zag of halls, ENSA arrangements and stars' canteens during wartime, or the continued battle for top-bookings in the early fifties. And before the war even began, you'd go where you were sent, tours worked out by Moss or whatever agency you were with, and never itinerary of towns near each other.

"Blackpool one night and Land's End the next, no wonder Max Miller only plays where he can get home from," one of the old comics once said to Court. As Sid Field had it, "What a performance!"

Court'd voiced concerns about the ribbon-cuttings when next having Sunday tea at Grandwem's.

"You beggars never know whether you're coming or going," said Grandwem, "you're as confused as a Wildew."

"A what, Win?"

"A Wildew. You know. Wildew doesn't know if he's Sid or Sadie."

"Ma, if you mean those people who are supposedly born as both men and women," said Billy, who'd clearly had the conversation before, "I'll mek it easy for you. They don't exist."

"They do. Mrs Hills had one."

"So, let me get this right," said Court, "someone in Mansfield had a kid born with both men's and women's private-bits."

"Ah. At least that's what folk said. I didn't ask too much about down below. But I heard the parents had to choose, and one lot went and the other stayed."

"So what were they in the end?"

"A girl. Betty Hills. But, sad to say she always looked a bit masculine. I think they got rid of the wrong bit. Stride like a docker. Never married. Drove a bus during the war."

"And now?"

"Oh, she died. Did away wi' her sen. Mrs Hills never got over it, once told me she was meant to be a boy, and her and Mr Hills made a mistake. 'I wanted a girl, so I chose, but she never was comfortable in her skin,' she said, as if I knew all the ins-and-outs of it.'"

"All that, if Wildew existed, which it doesn't, load of old nonsense." Said Billy.

"She did exist," said Grandwem crossly, "and seemed to be both. Then one, but the wrong one."

"Both! I ask you, Courtney, this town's full of daft stories!" Billy wouldn't have it, so that was the end of that conversation.

Whatever the truth, or not, behind the unfortunate Betty Hills, Grandwem had hit the nail over the head about Court and Billy not knowing if they were coming or going – a subject they came back to later in the evening. "I miss the old days, and I know we're lucky," Court said, "we're top of the tree and riding-high."

It was the smell of dressing rooms – spilt powder, leather strapped cases, Pond's Cold Cream, and brown ale – that he

144

missed most... Stage Hands and Call Boys you'd seemed to have known forever... he tried not to think of horror stories in the papers:

ONE OF THE OLDEST HALLS – A SAM TORR FREE AND EASY – BURNS TO GROUND

VARIETY HALL TO HOST BINGO EVENTS

ALHAMBRA PULLED DOWN – LAST SHOW A NUDE REVIEW

Hand-tinted turns gracing Court's postcard collection would have played some of those fast-disappearing halls, and stories of old theatres for the chop or reaching fiery ends were becoming all too common. Fires seemed everywhere, and if not arson, then it was destruction by councils anxious for newly released land on which to build supermarkets, shopping precincts and squares. Incredible, really, he and Billy were lucky to have the telly.

He thought, often, of Mighty Rosco's small Nottingham house, whose peeling exterior concealed a collection of music hall *objets d'art* and memorabilia, that was unparalleled as far as Court could see. Rosco had wanted his stuff saving for posterity, but, so far, several museums had rejected the idea of being left the collection. "It's the people's history, they've loved, laughed and cried with us, over the years, but no bogger wants it in a glass case. They look at me and see something down-market. I suppose I don't blame them."

Courtney was in talks on Rosco's behalf with the Victoria and Albert museum to take-on some of the collection, where it would be added to a growing archive they already had, but the process was a long one, and Rosco was losing heart. "I want it seen as a living thing," he said, "not in a basement somewhere."

Plaster cherubs and swagged roses... costumes in fading velvet and gilt-cord that once belonged to the likes of Dan Leno... Court hoped Rosco, old as he was becoming, was still collecting and not standing still, fretting over what he had. If he took buses and trains from place to place, surely Rosco might salvage something of what was being destroyed?

The story almost cracking Court's heart was one that had made the middle pages of Midlands' papers. This told an (after-the-event) tale of The Royal Leicester, the biggest hall outside London, and in its day the most luxurious. Built in 1904, it had been demolished within two weeks, despite the designer being Frank Carnaby, architect to stars and royals. Carnaby who'd once designed a summer-house for the great Houdini, and offices for some of the country's biggest trade halls. His masterpiece reduced to small square chunks of rubble.

It had all gone... Moorish tiles... rockeries with fountains and small falls of water... murals of "Eastern" princesses... all knocked down without so much as a plush seat saved. Court hoped Rosco'd turned up to rescue something, even if it was only a carved mask from a balcony. Yet the demise of the place had been so gingerly reported, Court doubted there'd've been time.

In his head, he'd heard the querulous tones of Vesta Victoria; "There was I, waitin' at the church," and saw a small figure in a long gown confronting a laughing crowd. The song echoed as he'd looked at newspaper photographs of rubble over which the heading went:

PEOPLE'S PALACE GOES UNDER THE WRECKING BALL.

A sad, shabby selection of photographs, reverberating to: "All at once, he left me in the lurch, Lord, how it did upset me!" Wreckage was smashed wedding-cake icing, trodden underfoot. A real mess.

The night at Grandwem's (after the conversation about someone who may, or may not have been, a Wildew, if that state existed) saw Court turning back to how lucky he and Billy were, but how difficult it was to know if you were coming or going. "Just carry on," Grandwem had said. 'That's all any of us can do.'

After, he went to bed at Shirl and Alf's and dreamed of Rosco dragging lumps of Moorish plaster from a big building, as a wrecking-ball swung above him.

It was a dream Court would have again, the small figure lumbering like a wasp on sponge-cake, just before it found a glass of beer to fall into... velvet-clad seats coated in layers of plaster dust... and the picture of fountains silting, un-visited in lobbies... awaiting being next. They said you couldn't hear dreams, and yet, when Court woke it was with a voice that had been singing in his sleep... "Here's the very note... this is what he wrote... 'can't get away to marry you today, my wife, won't let me!'"

Vesta Victoria, singing on, and loud enough, he thought, to wake the dead.

SMASHING TIME.

150

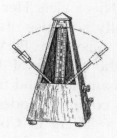

Mr Illuminator

It was all over the papers –

COOPER AND BEAN TOP VIEWERS' POLLS – PAIR AS BIG AS ERIC AND ERNIE

And all over the local press –

OUR LAD DONE GOOD (WITH A LITTLE HELP FROM HIS FRIEND!)

Beryl was also in the middle and back of the locals, and even on page two of *Variety Now*:

COSTUMIER LANDS TOP JOB AT LONDON'S DELAMERE CLUB, DRESSING THE FAMOUS DE VERE DANCERS AND, ALSO, LANDS HER MAN!

The local one being an announcement in the engagements column:

Mrs Winifred Bean and her husband, George, are pleased to announce the engagement of their Grand-daughter, Miss Beryl Potter, costumier, to Mr Ernest Fields, singer. The wedding will take place at the beginning of next year, at Saint Mod's Chapel, Mansfield, and afterwards at the Bell Inn, Newstead, an occasion hosted by Mr Billy Bean and Mr Courtney Cooper.

They were also in the *Town Talk* section, under the heading "Our Billy's Niece Gets Her Man." This was an article that was basically a reprise of the Cooper and Bean story, rather than a piece on Beryl and Ernie. Still, Grandwem thought the picture of the happy pair with Courtney and Billy "champion" and framed both that page, and the engagements column. Indeed, her and George's hallway had become a gallery of Cooper and Bean. "You can't saunter towards the lavvy without our mugs grinning at you," as Billy had it, "Steady on, Ma!"

Meanwhile, the costumier who'd landed her man was fretting on several counts, giving her sleepless nights. On a personal count, Beryl wondered if she should tell Ernie about Little Rita's true parentage. He hadn't coughed-up with an engagement ring yet, and telling him when he did would sour the atmosphere, and, she thought, would probably see him snatching it back.

On the work front, Big Webbly Jones of the *New Beat* tour had requested she design a suit for him, and not just any suit, but one that lit-up on stage! She'd never done, and seldom heard of, such a costume. Researching the history of similar endeavours, which was patchy at best, she realised she'd need to recruit a lighting expert, if she'd any hope of success. To top it all, Big Webbly specified (in the same letter making the request) that the suit should look stylish "and not what I believe you English call tacky." How could an illuminated suit not look "tacky", wondered Beryl. In the same letter, Big Webbly had noted that many of his fans in England were sharply dressed "modernists" who would accept lighting only if it looked "cool and artistic, like coffee bars in Italy."

So, these were her bugbears –

To tell Ernie or not.

If she did she'd rub up against the advice and wishes of her whole family.

If she didn't, her husband-to-be would be marrying (to use local parlance) "soiled goods" without knowing.

If told, he might chuck her.

If not, he might find out and chuck her after they'd married. Or, they'd stay together and resent each other...

... And she'd seen them, the loveless unions or ones that never quite clicked. Women with cigarettes dangling as they stared into the middle distance of smoky ladies' lounges while their blokes played darts, or worse, sat in the bit that used to be blokes only, chatting to semi-interested men who weren't their husbands...

Ernie hadn't given a ring yet, but said he was planning a "big surprise" on their next mutual day off, which Beryl both anticipated and dreaded. "Ernie's choosing me a ring," she said to Grandwem, hoping she'd hear the rising panic in her voice, but to which the reply came: "I hope it's sunny as his smile."

In the meantime, it was the problem of Big Webbly's suit. She could do a great suit, and knew it. But next to the De Vere Dancers, who looked a doddle, the electric suit was a conundrum and the more she read, the less Beryl conned of electrics. Luckily, Billy found a man who did, but he was a strange fish. An older man, who struck Beryl at first meeting as being like a daddy doll from a doll's-house-set (neat tie, old-fashioned suit, and a face that, despite the wrinkles round his eyes, looked like a smooth plastic mask). And he spoke in a strange sing-song. "Lighted suit, eh? Haven't done one of those babies in an age. You see, in my day, that would've brought the house down. No mistaking it.

"You see, at the end of the First War (I was invalided out, like our Billy and Courtney in the Second) I had an act, *Mr Illuminator and his Modern Marvels*. Of course, it'd be no marvel these days. Electric gets under-used in my book, despite all the stage lighting done to look like night clubs - but in those days, anything lit in a new way seemed quite something.

"You see, Miss Potter, the trick was I touched objects on stage (a standard lamp, a statue...) and they glowed with electric light. And I put paint on the shades and edges, paint that was luminous. They went mad for it. The band played a suitable tune, something about moonlight, and I lit the stage bit by bit. The real finale, of course, was dogs."

"Dogs?"

"Oh yes, Miss Potter, little bulbs in their collars and luminous paint on their nose-ends. Big dogs, borzois, right down to a Jack Russell, 'dignity and impudence.' Five dogs of varying sizes on a luminous see-saw. Quite something. Of course, I hired the dogs season-to-season. Not really the doggy type."

"So, that was a long time ago, and could you still do it? Not the dogs, but could you light Big Webbly's suit? Safely?"

"Safely. In all my years, I never lost a dog."

They sat in silence for a moment and then Mr Illuminator said: "Do you want a shape in the back, they went mad for Blackpool Tower in the old days."

"What about a thinly silhouetted guitar, sort of abstract?"

"Splendid."

154

Beryl had found a postcard with an image of Mr Illuminator, in Courtney's collection. To her, apart from the slight wrinkles around the eyes he boasted now, he looked unchanged. He stood in dinner dress and holding a standard lamp. There was a silver-topped cane in the picture, resting in the hand without the lamp.

"Oh, yes," he'd recalled during their conversation, "I limped more in my heyday. I don't bring my stick out much, Miss Potter. Funnily enough, the leg they've given me now means I can go without aid much of the time. But then, I was fitted with a real tin one. I lost mine in 1915. They've done wonders in the years since.

"Still, I needed the cane anyway, for proof I wasn't a battle-dodger. Even limping there used to be a cry: 'why aren't you at the front, Sonny?' That young Sandy Powell really got it in the neck, even though he wasn't of an age to fight. They had to put his birth certificate in foyers to prove he was under conscription age. Still, makes you think … Now he's 'Mr Eastbourne' and I'm retired and in an advisory capacity only. He still does panto you know. I miss it …"

Beryl contrived two suits, one sky, and one two-tone. Both with black and abstract guitar designs on the back – sky blue for matinees and the other for evenings. The strings of the guitar, lit by miniscule bulbs, followed the course of Big Webbly's spine. Sleeves also had tiny bulbs along the seams, as did the trousers, which were slightly flared. The jacket was large on the waist, to hide the electric's workings, and large lapels made Big Webbly's sizeable frame seem a little reduced. This Beryl had to alter after the singer saw the prototype: "I'm Big Webbly, Ma'am, Big! If anything, give me more stature, Man!" It was the first time a performer ever asked Beryl to make them look larger.

"Do you think Two-Ton Tessie O'Shea wants 'more stature'?" Beryl said to Billy.

"I certainly do, I never met anyone happier in their skin."

"Oh, well, then I'll 'give him more stature, Man!'"

By the time that Mr Illuminator got the suits ready to wire up, they'd gone through a significant number of changes, and he made alterations again to allow for his workings. Both Beryl and Big Webbly were sworn to secrecy as to how things actually-worked.

On opening night, when Big Webbly took to the stage, at Blackpool (where Beryl and Ernie were having their first weekend away together, in separate hotel rooms, so she assured Grandwem) Beryl's nerves were at a peak. She'd get her engagement ring the day following Big W's opening night, she knew it. In the theatre-box next to them, Mr Illuminator glowed with pride. As Big Webbly roared and shook, bringing the house down, he said: "That suit looks mint on its own, Miss Potter. Wait 'till they grasp the finale."

Beryl's heart pounded: What if the lights went down and nothing happened?

What if Ernie gave her the ring and she blurted out about Little Rita?

WHAT IF? WHAT IF? WHAT IF?

Lights went down. The band slowed. The auditorium was plunged into black velvet. There was a murmur. Not a power cut! Beryl and Ernie leant forward in as much anticipation as the rest. You could've heard a Spangle being sucked, Ernie later told Grandwem.

The stage was alight with a guitar made of stars.

A turn on the singer's part and the suit shimmied and snaked on its own. Stage became galaxy. Big Webbly turned, his face appearing as a lit mask. The audience went crackers: "We're a big smash, a smash-bang-hit!" Said Mr Illuminator, contentedly.

"Bugger it!" Thought Beryl. "If I can have a hand in this, an illuminated modernist suit, and come out smiling, without a duff bulb, I can weather bloody anything."

She took Ernie's hand and squeezed it, as the crowd continued to go wild.

In a box, further along, Ava Costain gasped along with the best of them. "Well, I'll be damned," she said. "Tour manageress and Big Webbly never told me. He didn't do it at rehearsals! Must've paid top-dollar from his own pocket! Nathan'll have a fit! Until he sees the reaction for himself. I never saw the like - Still, only one problem, now. How do we possibly bloody top this?"

Little Flames

"Bastard! I have-to get out! I don't usually travel in the van, as you know, and I *have to* get out!"

Big Webbly Jones thought he'd seldom encountered something as incongruous as Mrs Nathan Costain in the first of the three tour vans. The vans were decrepit, looking as if they'd seen war service, and Mrs Costain usually travelled in a plush car, a day in advance. But circumstances proved exceptional. They'd lost Slim du Val, guitarist, to rival management, who'd promised him a featured slot. He'd left in the night, and Mrs Costain was furious (livid at breakfast, with anger mounting as the morning stretched before them). She said she needed to travel with them to "sort the line-up" before they got to where they were going.

So far, they'd seen so many towns, Big Webbly found it hard to recall just where they were headed. South again, after Blackpool, that was for certain. He had Bournemouth in mind, or was it Eastbourne? Anyhow, it would be too chilly for him. Too chilly in the van, too, with Mrs Costain's range of still-unfamiliar British swear words falling through those near perfect pink-iced lips.

Her pale mink looked ridiculous squashed-up between musicians on the van's tattered seats. And then there were

159

patent-black heels with winkle-picker toes drumming on the rusty metal floor.

"Let me out!"

"We can't pull up yet. There's no lay-by." Said Bob, the driver.

"Well next bloody lay-by, God almighty!"

"Look, Mrs Costain," said Big Webbly, "we can do without Slim, that boy always thought he was better than he was. There's other guitar men, and sweeter."

"Not for tonight, and no one does a runner, or pulls a fast one on Gilda Graeme's time."

The unfamiliar name seemed to float in the air like steam from a coffee. "Gilda who?" Asked Big W.

"Oh, nothing. An old English expression, my mistake."

"I never heard that one 'Gilda Graeme's time'" said Bob, who was fond of an old saying.

"Haven't you found that friggin' lay-by yet?"

"Still looking, no need to get shirty."

"I wasn't."

Silence. Big Webbly often wondered if Mrs Costain was hiding something, she looked the type. An evasive expression in her eyes you caught on occasion or, as now, a name on her lips that seemed not to belong.

"Bugger Slim! He's for a right pasting next time we light on that shitty little weasel."

If Big Webbly suspected something odd about Mrs Costain, the woman was so fearsome he was going to let it lie, especially given her colourful turn of phrase and rapidity of temper-loss.

"Oi! There's a lay-by, a bloody lay-by, pull over, Bob."

"All right, you're the boss."

"I am, and I'm that angry!" They stopped at the lay-by, and got out of the van to stretch their legs, and hope Mrs Costain calmed down. There seemed slender hope of it.

"Ere," she said, "are there any of Slim's instruments left in the van?"

"No, ma'am, and anyway, no matter what hostility you feel, you shouldn't take-it-out on a man's guitar. It done nothin' to you," said Big W, feeling the heat.

"I don't care, don't bleedin' care. What has he left in the van?"

"Nothing, we're sure," came a chorus of voices fearing for their own dark instrument cases.

"You certain about that?"

"Well, Mrs Costain," Mike Charm (not his real name) a saxophonist, said from the back, "there is his new jacket."

Big W could have slapped Mike Charm, who he neither liked nor trusted. Charm, he felt, had that sly face you could come across in any small town, a smiling wild dog of a face. Features of a man who wasn't part of some nasty organisation up-front, but who ran to them with tales to tell soon as your back was turned.

"Now, Mike," said Big W, kind as he could muster, "that's not real friendly, a man's jacket can be his stage signature, like my new electric coat. Anyway, I'm sure Slim took his jacket away with him."

"Not the new one, he forgot it, it's still in the suit bag in the back."

"Even so," said Webbly, "a man's new jacket? I recall Slim saved and paid top-dollar for it, from Harry J. Belmont, 'Tailor to the Stars.'"

"Oh," said Ava Costain, "is that what Harry's calling himself these days? He was 'Harry Green, Spiv to the Many,' in good old Soho during the war."

Big Webbly was unsure of the term "Spiv", but felt he was getting Mrs Costain's icy drift. He gazed at the lay-by, it looked like every other lay-by where the boys'd stopped to shake the snake. A malnourished row of firs and some patchy grass. Had it been on a highway back home, there'd have been a hot-dog stand abandoned to the elements and racoons. No birds singing... just like there'd been a war ...

"Give me the jacket someone, take it out of the bag and give it to me," the pink-nailed hand was outstretched.

"Now steady on, Mrs Costain," someone said, "it's actual fake shark-skin, is that."

"I won't say it again, open the bag and give it here."

There was a shi-shing sound as someone un-zipped the bag, followed by a murmur of "right about the shark-skin, mate." The pale green, drape-style jacket was passed from musician to musician, finally reaching Big Webbly. He handed it to Mrs Costain himself, like the flag of a defunct regiment.

"Thank you boys," she said. Searching her elegant black crocodile bag, Mrs Costain produced a gold Colibri lighter, with "AC" picked-out in diamonds, topped by a pair of red enamel lips, the same shape as her own. A gift from Nathan on her last birthday. Mrs Costain knew the price of something you paid "top dollar" for.

She held the pale green jacket, with its oddly crunchy fabric, at arm's length. Even she had to admit, it would look good on stage, losing the hunched shape it had when empty. Then Ava Costain considered the label:

"Belmont – Tailor to the Stars, hand-made."

"You sly old devil, Harry,' she whispered, before holding his creation at arm's length, clicking the Colibri until a small gilt flame emerged flickering against the chill, and setting light to the sleeve bottom.

Realising it was taking quickly, she cast the flaming jacket at the firs beyond.

As they watched it twist and burn, Big Webbly realised a fir was also going to catch. He went back to the van, grabbed a fire-extinguisher, and did the necessary.

"That," he said, "was not cool."

Ava Costain looked him up and down with the triumph of someone grinding the ring given by an unpleasant suitor underfoot.

"No one messes with me, no one," she said, walking back to the van without a second glance at the charred heap below the trees.

Big Wheels

"Don't you flamin' take him on the wheel, not after all that rubbish you bin' feedin' 'im."

"Oh, come on, Maureen, the little perisher wants to get on. He's been lookin' forward all afternoon!"

"He's had pop, toffee apple, candy-floss, and that green thing we weren't sure of."

"The man said it was a rock all-day-breakfast, but all I can say is, if it was, it was missing a few rashers," said her husband, sheepishly.

"A green breakfast! More like a dog's dinner, why'd you buy it for him, Maxie?"

"It wasn't me, it was your Ma, before she went back to the digs."

"Don't say 'digs' it's common, say 'guest house.'"

"All right, before she swanned off to the bleedin' guest house! Look, he's fine, aren't ya, kid? Wants to go on the big wheel. Don't you? 'Bin lookin' forward."

"Yeah," the boy said, managing to sound both sticky and uncertain, "looking forward." He smiled, but whey features told a different story. The young couple in the queue in front of Beryl and Ernie had a hand each, seeming in danger of cleaving their offspring in two.

"He won't be sick, will you Albert? He's a chip off the old block, can stand anything. He's robust."

"Robust my eye, Maxie, he looks pasty. Just like you after a night on the tiles. Well, I'm not getting in with him looking like that. If his stomach misbehaves, they'll say it reflects on us, as parents. There's been enough stories in the news about the younger generation not coping, without us fuelling the fire…"

By now, the young couple had reached the front, with the queue behind listening in. "The girl's right," said a woman a few couples back, "the press won't let this generation alone, makes you wonder what we fought a war for. They're entitled to a bit of a giggle."

"So long as that lad don't giggle yellow over the seat," said her husband, "looks nauseous to me."

"Blimey," Ernie said, "there'll be another war if this carries on."

"HE'S GOIN' AND THAT'S FINAL!" the man yelled. "AND I'M GOIN' TOO. WE'LL ENJOY OURSELVES AWAY FROM THE BLEEDIN' HOITY-TOITY GUEST HOUSE."

"Like he's swallowed a fog-horn," said Ernie, as the wife strode past him, near to tears, "I hope we never get like that."

By the time the man reached the ticket booth, at least three couples had pushed past him, one old fella saying, "You meks your mind up, or you loses your place."

"Go, on," said Ernie to the man, "you next, we're not pushers-in."

"Ernie?" Beryl was pale as the disputed-over boy.

"What?"

"Do we have to go on the big wheel?"

"Yes, we do, course we do, don't let them put you off. Besides, I have something for you, and it would be nicer with a panoramic view of Blackpool below us."

"Oh!"

Conversation was curtailed as the man and boy had purchased tickets, the man insisting they went to the front of the queue for seats, angering the pushers-in, and now rendering at least three compartments between himself and the boy, and Beryl and Ernie. "When he's on top, we're on bottom," Ernie laughed. As parting shot at his wife, the man waved tickets in the air with demeanour of an Olympic athlete.

His spouse, now on the queue's outskirts, was heard to shout "FINE, I HOPE IT KEEPS BLEEDIN' FINE FOR YOU, MAXIE SWIFT."

She raced back to where he was in better earshot. "I HOPE IT KEEPS FINE!" Then, turning to Beryl and Ernie she said, in more subdued manner, "Kids! Don't ever do it, they ruin your life. I was Miss Winter Gardens twice in a row, twice! Now look at me, arguing over a stupid joy-ride!"

Beryl's insides did a cha-cha-cha as she and Ernie settled themselves in the bottom-smoothed seats. He was fiddling with his upper-pocket, which could mean only one thing, a ring box. She pondered how, when things were meant to be fun, doom-laden notices always abounded:

PLEASE KEEP FEET AND HANDS WITHIN THE COMPARTMENT.

DO NOT SWING OR LEAN OUT TO EXCESS.

NO ALCOHOL PERMITTED ON RIDE.

NO LARKING ABOUT.

To this, Beryl mentally added, "AND IF YOU WERE MISS WINTER GARDENS TWICE RUNNING, NO ARGUING OVER A STUPID JOY-RIDE."

Ernie settled down. "Not bad, this,' he said, "we'll be starting off in a minute."

Beryl gulped as the wheel cranked into action and they rose. She'd agreed to marry him, thus didn't have to answer a proposal, so why did she suddenly feel like climbing out before the ride got too high?

"We go-round three times, I asked," he said.

From above, they could catch the boy's dad shouting "Wooo... wooo... This is the life! We'll prove your Ma wrong yet!"

Then, suddenly, his voice vanished on the wind, and Beryl and Ernie were at the top.

She could see the Pleasure Beach laid out below like something from a Hornby set, people small as lead figures. The boy's mother was somewhere down there, fuming.

"Beryl?" Said Ernie.

"Yes." She heard the flatness in her voice and felt ashamed, knowing this was everything to him.

"Since we got engaged, I've felt like I do up here all the time, miles high. I was saving this" (he took a blue leather box from the top-pocket) "and now, I want you to have it. But first, I have to tell you something that may change your mind about us."

"What is it?" The compartment swung, as did the view, ready for their descent. Serves me right, Beryl thought, all this worry, and he's been playing away.

"Well, it's just that, I don't care about your past. All I want is our future. I know there's something you haven't told me. Someone who loves you, as much as I do, said so. But... you should know... I don't care. I had nothing when I was growing up, and I'm not sorry, that's just how it was. But with you, now, I have everything, and I'd never turn it away, for something done and dusted."

Beryl's eyes pricked, feeling sore at the edges. Ernie handed her the suddenly opened box and through blurring she saw a lovely ring. Perfect. Three circles and three diamonds of varying size. Older rather than new, but just her style. She took it from the box, which she gave-back to Ernie to replace in his pocket, and said, "Put it on me; I'll never take it off."

"Wooo... Wooo..."

The boy and his dad must be below them, ready to go back up. The ring was a sparkler on her finger, she was glad she'd had her nails painted Bonfire Red.

The wheel turned again and they were going towards the base. Their second turn. "Thank you," she said, and then, "Was it Grandwem that told you?"

SPLAT!

A comedy cow-pat of spew covered their feet. The stench was like a sugar factory that'd caught fire.

"You little bleeder!" Yelled Ernie, leaning out. Beryl pulled him in. He was beside himself. Someone being sick on you and your intended after a ring was given never happened in Rock Hudson films. "That little weasel! He must be above us, and he's leant out and been ill. I bet there's nothing in their seats!"

"Urgh. It's all over our shoes," said Beryl, "You got a hankie?"

"One."

"Well, I've got a bag full of toilet paper."

"How come?"

"Grandwem swears by it, never goes anywhere without a half box of Izal, just in case."

"Good on her."

"Says you never know when you'll be caught-short, or the dog…"

The harsh, grease-proof textured sheets could only clean so much. But it was better than nothing. "We're going up again, we can't chuck it off after we've cleaned, that'll put some other poor sods in our position," Ernie said, adding, "Suppose we can bundle them up in a corner and explain when we get off. Oh, bogger it, Beryl, I just thought of something."

"What?"

"They'll think it's us. Down there. That lad'll get off without a stain, and his old man's hardly the confessional type. And I wanted this to be perfect!"

"Well, it may not be perfect, but it's certainly memorable. But you might want to chuck me after all."

"Why?"

"Because 'bogger it' 's a phrase of Alf's, shows you've been visiting Mansfield too long."

"I love you, Beryl Potter, and your mad family. I'm part of their world now, just like they chant in that old *Freaks* film: 'one of us… one of us…'"

"That got banned."

"Yeah, but when I worked for Karniko, we got an illegal showing. Horrible it was, but had nothing on this sick."

"Oh, Love,' she said, 'none of this matters. You've told me you don't care about the past, only about now. Well, sick cleans up, and explanations can be made, and besides, I've got a beautiful new ring."

By the time the wheel had done a rotation that, as was predicted, let sick boy and his dad off scot-free, Beryl and Ernie were ready for the ire to come when it was their turn to get off. It was a good job they hadn't heard the guard's comment to the man and his son. "Eh, boys, you've had the best Blackpool's had to offer, now why don't you get a stick of rock each and a bottle of pop?"

Long as she lived, Beryl laughed at what happened next, although it took Ernie months to see the funny side.

"Well you dirty beggars," said the guard as they got off, "have you been on the ales? Old enough to know better – worse than something from the Monkey House! I should've put up a notice: DO NOT FEED THE APES."

"No, Sir," said Ernie, "you don't understand, a little lad was sick above us, he'd had lots of sweeties and fizz."

"Well, I call that criminal, blaming a nice little chap like that for your calumny. Hooligans! I saw that boy, clean as a whistle."

"But… " Ernie was beside himself.

"Sick on you, was he? A likely story."

"Come on, Ernie," Beryl spoke with as much dignity as someone with sick on their shoes could muster, "he clearly doesn't believe you, so let's go."

As they walked away they heard, "Get the brush and shovel Bernard, Monkey House again."

Once stockings and socks had been binned, and they'd visited separate loos to clean themselves, Beryl looked down at her ring, eyes welling. "I love my ring, and maybe sick's a lucky sign somewhere," she said.

Later that night, cleaned up and changed, they went to The Cottage for a late supper, munching through golden-battered cod and bright sticks of fried potato - Ernie saying it was one of the best feeds he'd ever had, right down to the tomato sauce.

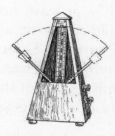

Sorting Things

Coals fallen from the fire, patterns in ash, tarot cards, fortune-tellers' cups, tea leaves, spirit-boards, voices from those gone... None of them could be avoided if a message was to be passed on ...

Grandwem knew she was sorting things out, just in case – her "just in case" seeming more urgent than it used to be now Norrie was no more.

Alf and Shirl had Little Rita to take care of. Ernie (though Grandwem would never own up as to how he found out) knew about Beryl's past lapse and didn't bloody care. Now he and Beryl were furnished with a ring, and Grandwem and Alf nearly choked on their chip cobs when told about the big wheel and the sick.

The cinema where she and George worked (as sweetie man and ticket seller) was doing famously, and they were content with their jobs. Then there was the continuing success of Courtney and Billy on television, where they'd even met The Beatles and Ken Dodd, it was champion! But, in Grandwem's experience, just when you thought life was chugging along, that was when the shadow people came calling, restless spirits who dogged you down the street, signalling change.

Grandwem was sure the feeling of "someone behind you in the pantry" she'd been having wasn't a presence that had come for her personally – at least, not yet. But something niggled, like green-mould spores on a piece of brown bread, and it was to do with Courtney. Sometimes, she caught him looking at Billy with a remorseful face. The lad was bottling summat up, make no mistake. Not that she'd seen much of either Courtney or Billy in past weeks, but that didn't stop her mithering.

She thought of the woman in grey she'd kept catching sight of, just before their Rita died. No one believed her, and then Rita had dropped dead while telling-off one of Beryl's teachers. They believed it then. Then there'd been Rita's ex-beau, Grandwem's "drowned man," ghost she'd seen visiting the town years ago, a reminder, she thought, of the life her daughter could have had with someone she cared for. She hoped, at least, Beryl and Ernie had the chance her Rita was denied.

The blue envelope resting on the sideboard seemed, to Grandwem, as portentous as her woman in grey and drowned man put together.

A letter on thin blue, Izal-textured paper, bearing Billy's name and address in print that resembled that of a kid's John Bull printing set. It meant no good, Grandwem was sure.

Usually, she left letters for Billy until he came home, but this one dwelt in its place as though a rancid smell came off it. Even the near-transparent paper offended her sight. It didn't matter where she placed the envelope, it seemed to smugly catch the corner of her eye.

"Open it, lass, find out what it is that's corroding the house!" Norrie's voice whispered to his sister. "A bad letter's more poisonous than a haunting, or summat off in the larder."

Eventually (loudly asking the absent Billy's forgiveness) Grandwem took her Dad's silver-plate letter-opener, topped with a brass rendition of a chorus girl's frilly-panted bottom, and sliced the envelope.

She stood by the lit fire to read. The letter was marked "from a well-wisher," its contents anything but. Unsigned. The words were produced by a John Bull letter set stamped onto the page and must have taken the perpetrator ages.

Dear Mr Billy Bean, it began, *it is from a position of fandom that I write. Despite your success, I believe some elements of life have eluded you, namely children and wedded bliss. I have news for you that reflects on this.*

("Ayup, some bogger with a grudge," Grandwem thought as she read on).

My news may shed new light on your comedy partner, Mr Cooper. It could, indeed, alter relations. To find out more, seek Mrs Ivy West at The Cricketers' public house, Brighton. I believe you once knew Mrs West intimately. Or, just ask Mr Cooper if the name 'Ted' rings any bells. Your servant – The Well Wisher.

An un-signing cowardly little weasel, by Grandwem's lights, and surely, she thought, by anyone's. Words had letters missing where print hadn't taken, and the whole job was smeary. As she read through again, she noted the strange, reedy tone. And that paper – truly like summat you'd wipe your nethers on!

Placing letter in pinnie pocket, Grandwem went and got a pencil, noting Ivy's address in her diary. Then, without a second thought, she put diary in pocket, and, withdrawing the letter, walked back to the fire and cast it in the flames. It made a satisfying crackle, and Grandwem swore if more missives followed they'd end the same way.

If the man (if it was a man) wrote directly to Billy, whatever he knew would have to emerge. She remembered, vaguely, Billy saying something about a man who got thrown off a show, who'd sent something nasty to him and Court, but on their last visit, they'd said his correspondence seemed to have ended, and the studio had been told to send any further communications to the police. In fact, Court added, the studio had issued some sort of warning in the theatrical press, and said, in future, bad mail wouldn't be tolerated.

Still, it made her wonder how someone got Billy's old home address. It bothered her an individual could find something like that out. But, their Billy's life was public now, all over the papers, and he'd been interviewed on television, too.

Noting Ivy's whereabouts, Grandwem went to the pantry, to see how last week's plum jam was settling in the pots...

*

Grandwem recalled Ivy as a sweet, harassed looking woman, who knew she'd never replace romantic-voiced Ruby in Billy's affections. As Grandwem headed towards The Cricketers' she noted the pub's pleasant façade with its rag-stone and dark brick edges, and the smart looking garage attached – Ivy must be doing all right to be running such a place. But if Ivy was doing all right, then Grandwem wasn't.

She thought of the whoppers she'd told all but George about her trip to Brighton.

In one lie, she was visiting Maddie Stansfield, an old friend she'd lost touch with, who'd invited her.

In lie two, Maddie was gravely ill and wanting to see Grandwem.

Lie three saw invalided Maddie sending her a ticket, so how could she refuse to go?

How had Maddie got their address, asked Shirl?

Through lie four, another old friend.

Should Shirl go with her? No. She wanted to go alone, and Shirl had Little Rita, who was getting bigger every day.

"The hugest lie of all?" Thought Grandwem. She'd never known a Maddie Stansfield but taken the name from Maddie's Advice column in *People's Choice* magazine, and Stansfield Tea, sitting on a shelf in the pantry.

Grandwem bothered the pub door ages before knocking. Too early for opening time. Eventually, Ivy opened up.

"Mrs Bean, why have you come?" She said, adding, "that sounded rude, I meant it's been a long time."

"Ah. It has that. Look, when you realise why I'm here, you might want to send me away again, I won't blame you. But, you see, I've had a nasty letter, or, rather, our Billy has."

"Oh God! He knows about Ted, doesn't he?"

"He knows nowt. To my shame, I opened the letter and read it. Now I've burned it. I've lied through me socks to get here, and will lie through them when I get back, apart from to George and the budgie."

Ivy's worn face curved into a smile, she realised she'd no war-paint on.

"I look a sight, but come in," she said, "Good grief, where's my manners? Truth is, I've had that bad a time of it, Mrs Bean, I don't know where I'm at. Ted's in prison, just so as you know why I never told Billy of him, proper prison this time, not somewhere for the young. He robbed some people of tickets outside a popular music concert not so long ago. When the man challenged, he slashed his arm... with a razor. Another man grabbed him, and the courts and that did him soon as they could. It wasn't a first offence, he's worked for gangsters and everything, soon as he could buzz-off from school."

"I see."

"Yes, that's the sort of boy I've had." She said as she and Grandwem climbed up to her sitting room, "although, I'd like to think I did my best. The man he slashed turned out to be a joiner, and what Ted did, ruined his livelihood. Decent, working people! Makes me hate meself."

"Now, now, Ivy. Some people are born bad." Grandwem sighed. "I can't imagine you bringing someone up to be a little waster."

*

Ivy and Grandwem sat over cups of tea and glasses of Grandwem's own plum brandy. Even though visiting a pub, Grandwem brought a hip-flask in her handbag, as she thought plum brandy might be needed. Plum brandy, plum wine and plum jam – they couldn't be beat!

"So," she said to Ivy, "were you telling me Ted's our Billy's son?"

"Yes.'"

"Born after he'd upped-sticks?"

"Yes."

"And you never wanted him to know, and get in on the act?"

"No, never. Go on! Call me wicked."

178

"Suppose I should. Still, in my book life's never as you think. Tell us, was Ted always a wrong 'un?"

The relief of talking about it saw tears stain Ivy's cheeks. "Rotten, always. A mother shouldn't say it of her own kid, but I will. Heaven knows, I tried, the school tried, and my mates tried. Something about him was mean... mean spirited... as time passed I couldn't believe someone like that could come from me and Billy, and your lot... And ... he's always sought out the like-minded."

"And Courtney knew about him?"

"Ted's first bout of trouble at school, was when Court was visiting. One night, I got blind drunk and spilled the beans. He's been lovely to me, you shouldn't blame him."

"Now, who says I do?"

"Court's wanted to tell Billy, God knows! But Billy loves him, and your Beryl's always idolised him, how could I spoil that?"

"I see why you didn't say."

"Look, it'd break Billy's heart. Ted's brung me nothing but remorse – I go to sleep thinking of that poor man he slashed. Courtney would suffer if I said, and for what? He's tried to help and Ted's always chucked it back."

"Ted has no inkling Billy's his Dad?"

"I told him his Dad died at the end of the war, Mrs Bean, and if it's all the same to you, that's how I intend to keep it. I'm carrying on here, but I've told him, when he gets out, he's to make his own way. I can't do this again."

Grandwem thought of the pale blue letter crisping on the fire. She smiled at Ivy. "Then I think we can agree Billy shan't know."

"But what if that man writes again?"

179

"I have a feeling that we won't hear, but if we do, then we may have to amend things. But, for now, I'm going home." She smiled at Ivy. "You know, Love, I doubt I shall come this way again. So, I'm calling on your neighbour on my travels. Agnes; we're friends of old. Come to think of it, I don't know why I didn't tell Shirl I was visiting her in the first place, instead of making up some old rope. Agnes was once in the films, you know."

Grandwem did as she said, and Ivy watched as the small figure in the mustard coat vanished into The Black Lion. Before putting on her make-up she decided to toast herself with the last of the plum wine, Grandwem having left the hip-flask behind as a souvenir.

A Taste of Plum Jam

Sometimes, Grandwem's spirits moved unexpectedly, a bit like images offered by a shuffled tarot. There could be a bad sign, or one that was good for you, but that signalled worse portents for another.

The "keep death off the roads" dark woman following their Rita all those years ago, had been bang on the money. Grandwem Win's daughter had died without ceremony, in front of a teacher at the school, and left Beryl motherless. And that ghost of Rita's former sweetheart, Grandwem's drowned man, what had he been, but thinned reminder of what could have been, had Rita lived? Now it was Norrie's turn, not long dead, and thus still bothering the air.

All the way back on the train from Brighton, Norrie's voice whispered to his sister: "That blue letter man, he can't tell no more, trust me, trust me, Gypsy Sayers says so."

She'd fall asleep, waking to, "Our Billy's better off now nothing's said, trust me."

Then, just as the train pulled in to Nottingham for her connection, the tones faded into air, and Grandwem knew her brother gone for good. She sniffed, but it was only right – he couldn't hang around for ever.

181

If only Grandwem could've read the story in the Worthing papers, she'd've known Norrie was, like her woman in grey, bang on the cash.

MAN FALLS UNDER HORSE-DRAWN ATTRACTION AT LOCAL SHOW – COMEDY PERFORMER DIES AT WORTHING'S CAVALCADE OF HISTORY.

Read the headline of one regional gazette. The piece continued:

A man dressed as a bottle of gin fell under horses drawing a traditional brewer's dray carrying Miss Worthing at the town's cavalcade.

It has been thought the local actor, known under the monika 'Gin-and-Tonic', performed regularly at Rapelli's Trattoria, Bexhill. Bystanders reported he'd been seen drinking at several establishments prior to the accident. Investigations are on-going, and police believe the individual went under several names, including Gerald Sym, which may or may not be his birth name.

It is, at present, considered inebriation coupled with self-promotion to be the principal elements that enabled the tragedy to happen. A police spokesman revealed to our reporter Mr Sym was wearing a singularly hampering costume, resembling a felt and plastic gin-bottle. It is believed the costume was all part of an advertising stunt which went wrong - Worthing councillors being quick to point out that Mr Sym was not employed as part of the pageant.

It is believed that Mr Sym's long-standing engagement with Rapelli's had come to an end with some bad feeling on his part. Those interviewed from his old employment recalled he had begun to "hector" customers concerning a lack of starring opportunities. They continued that, whilst they were sad he had come to such an untimely end, his demeanour gave them no choice but to terminate his employment.

Both police and journalists appear to have reached the same conclusion in this unusual case – namely, Mr Sym had grabbed at the horses' reins in costume, in order, to advertise his services to local venues. It seems likely he tripped and fell, and the cumbersome nature of the felt and plastic gin bottle meant he could not rise before the horses went over him.

Miss Worthing is said to be recovering at home, and a statement from the Council assures next year's cavalcade will continue as normal. Councillors have also made the unusual, but we think fair, decision, Miss Worthing can be granted another year in post, rather than give up her crown before next year's event, as is the norm.

It is hoped this will leave both her, and the crowds, with happy memories of their cavalcade and its queen.

*

A few months after her homecoming, Grandwem invited Courtney down for a visit, alone, and spoke privately to him, telling what she knew.

"I can't explain why, but I think that blue letter bogger's gone," she said, "Someone on the inside told me, and I believe it to be so. Now, do you want a jam sandwich and cuppa?"

"What do you mean he's gone? How can you know that, Win? You haven't even met him."

"It's plum jam, new. Lovely and thick with fruit, last of what was behind Norrie's caravan."

"But Win! That letter-writer, how do you know?"

"I know lots of things, like me jam will never taste sunny as this now me brother's no more. Like young folk are right to be dressing in flowery clothes, and wanting to mek the most of things. Sometimes, you know summat in yer wind, and it's best not to explain, just tek it at face value. Now, can you believe me?"

"I dunno. On past stuff, yeah, yeah, I suppose so."

"Good, then I'll get that jam butty, and while you eat up, I've summat to ask you."

The jam tasted sunny as Grandwem said. It was hedgerows, and late light, and tunes Court had whistled as a kid.

"Now you know those letters done and dusted, I may as well tell you ... I visited Ivy West in Brighton, and she and I talked. Over plum brandy, same plums as you're tasting now."

"So, that's what the sweetness is for, to sugar the bitter pill. You know about Ted, don't you? And you think I should've said. Bloody hell, Win!"

"I know, but Ivy told me you fair wanted to tell Billy. I don't blame you for not, she made you swear."

"Wasn't my fault," Court had turned red as a little lad caught opening the hamster's cage.

"Now, I've weighed things up. I came to a decision, that I've spoken over with Ivy. I wasn't going to contact her again, but I needed her agreement, so I telephoned."

Court thought of Grandwem standing on tip-toe and bellowing down the receiver. He smiled, in spite of things.

"Now past events are done, Ivy says she's cutting Ted from her life. When he comes out of prison, he's by his sen. I'm not sure I believe that's how things'll stay, but that's what she intends. Now, to me decision. You'll not like it, Courtney, but I don't want you to see Ivy more."

"What?"

"She's agreed to it, and thinks it best. Not ever again, Courtney, mind. Oh, and if you agree, none of us are ever going to say a word to Billy about Ted. That's for the best, too."

"But, why, Win? I'll have to live with a lie, not telling Billy. And if I don't see Ivy, the poor girl'll be on her own."

"I know, it bothers me, but can't be helped. Look, if Billy finds out now, it'll ruin all you've both worked for. He'll not forgive you for years, if ever, and Ivy can't live with that. Ted's made her life miserable, and she doesn't want him in Billy's doing the same. Can you respect that?"

"I suppose."

"Good lad. Now do you promise. Do you swear on your talent?"

"I swear."

"Proper."

"I swear on my talent."

"And Little Rita."

"And Little Rita."

"That's me boy. Now, you've had your jam-butty, there's some scones and cream in the pantry, go and get them, and I'll get a glass of sloe-gin, to toast the last of Norrie's bounty."

MEET YOUR WORLD

Good Times Rolling In

Nathan Costain was about to surprise Ava. The man who adored surprising folk, looked at his mighty handsome reflection in the hotel mirror. Even by his own lights, the boy looked sharp! Pressed shirt, knotted tie, pearl pin and links. He thought of his Daddy's words. "Look good, even when they got you on the ropes, and no man will match you. You solid gold!"

Shirt - hyacinth blue - tie - bold black and white diamond print. Oh, yeah, he had sharp in spades. "I look like I got a firm date," he laughed, going to pour himself a whisky. Champagne would have to wait. He'd ordered two bottles, and the whisky, from downstairs. The bus-boy who brought them on a silver salver had eyes on stalks when he saw Nathan's get-up. "You're that Mr Costain, Sir, of the *New Beat* tour … in the papers."

"I am that, Bud."

"Wait until I tell them at home, I served you. I'm sorry to be forward, Sir, but we're all ever so excited here."

"So am, I, Bud, so am I. If you watch your TV. when you get home, I'll be on *Pop It!* In a couple of night's time."

"Well, Sir, we don't have a TV at my house, my Gran, who I live with, says they give-off bad rays."

"And that's your Grandmother? Of the generation that's supposed to be wise?" Nathan chortled. "I'm sorry, Boy."

"No. You're right. I can watch it in the staff rest room."

"Like a 'toilet'?"

"Oh, no, like a room you rest in."

"Right. Well I'll tell them you have to watch it, you my best fan." Nathan tossed the boy a large note. The boy blanched. "'I have no change, Sir. I'll have to go downstairs."

"No change needed, Son. Just serve me well, the time I'm here." Nathan knew the value of tipping. It meant smooth service and a matchless reputation. And, if you were broke... well, no one need know, unless it all crashed down. Balancing those balls in the air, that was his speciality.

With Ava beside him, he could throw them higher, dazzle the crowd. Ava! How the name suited. Damn! He thought. Everything seemed to suit that woman – the red hair he'd had her bleach, the cut of the expensive suits he encouraged her to wear, and either pink-frosted lipstick that matched the times, or that ruby red he'd first admired her in. All of them seemed to go with her style. To his surprise, given his past track-record of flitting from one fine gal to the next, Nathan had been faithful to Ava. More than that, he'd come to England early because he missed her, much as for the deals he'd sorted. Rare for him, he hoped she'd been faithful. But, as his Daddy would've pointed out, you couldn't blame the hen for doing what the cock done first.

From her wide smile to that spitfire temper, maybe especially because of her lash of hell-cat, he'd missed it all. So as soon as opportunity for Big Webbly's London recordings came Nathan's way, he was on a plane. Oh, yeah, for once in his cheatin' life, he'd got it bad.

Of course, he'd come in on the best ticket, with no one in front row seats calling him "boy", even if he'd got a few stink-eyes from solid looking types who thought plenty, he knew, but refrained from voicing it.

Increasingly, he and Ava were getting known, and that opened doors and shut mouths. He'd had champagne and smoked-salmon on the flight, salmon decorated like it was at its own jazz funeral. He was served by girls in azure uniforms, charmed by his mile-wide smile. Nathan had chosen his sky-blue travelling suit with care.

He'd seen Elvis Presley wear similar, years ago, and had sought out Elvis's man, Bernard Lansky, for an updated version. How the blue clung like cut sky; damn, he could out-shine Elvis! Ava having told him the saga of Big W's electric-suit made him grin, in sky-blue this boy needed no light-bulbs.

Nathan circled the whisky glass until his drink rolled, a trapped sea. He considered their progress. The tour was doing well, reviews were great, places panted for new bookings, and old dates asked them to return. Pop art and word of mouth, were giving them publicity you couldn't buy. He'd started to keep a leather scrapbook of cuttings. Nathan recalled how once, when starting out, he'd met Louis Armstrong, who'd showed him his pages of cuttings. That must've been ten years ago, at least.

Nathan had been hanging around a recording studio, willing to fetch coffee, booze, or anything that would keep him there. The great man was passing by, and had gone to look up an old friend. He'd asked for ice tea, and Nathan had run to the diner and back like his life depended on it.

Mr Armstrong had smiled that huge railroad-track of a beam on Nathan, and said, "Pass me that bag, my man, I want you to see my dreams." Nathan passed the bag, and his hero had taken out a smart leather folder. Inside were sheets getting dog-eared at the edges. Opening it at the middle, he'd shown Nathan cuttings unlike any scrapbook he'd ever seen. "Don't know what I'll do with 'em, but they sure building-up," he said. The magazine and paper clippings revealed events, friends, and places, but cut, drawn-on, and coloured in fizzing yellows, pinks, and oranges, so they seemed like the best art in the world.

Looking at that folder was one of those things that happened to you, seeming so unreal, it was like it happened to someone else. "There you go, all my dreamin'" said Mr Armstrong, as he shut the folder and put the bag away.

"All my dreamin," Nathan repeated. Dreamin' was fine if you were King Louis, but he and Ava were still in the red. And, he thought wryly, how did he know King Louis wasn't in the red, too? After all, for most of them in the music business, life was one big Hollywood billboard, picture of a star up-front, but big wooden supporting-poles with garbage blowing round the legs at the back. Still, at least they had potential for money to roll in …and roll out… first-class dining for him, Ava, and the occasional headliner, vans at the rear and the big cars out front. He'd hire American, a Cadillac or two should do it, the big car on the small road … the exotic fin cruising the tightly-packed red-brick street. Top class flights, and a walk down a white gang-plank in immaculate dress… great hotels for showy exits and entrances … He knew Ava occasionally rode in the van, but that had to stop under his watch. "Show them the money you don't have, Boy, white fish out front, grits in private," his Daddy had laughed.

They'd do it for show, all or nothin' at all, like Sinatra sang. Performers got as little as Nathan could get away with paying. After all, the music men, songwriters and promoters took chunks, too. Nathan felt bad about his musicians' income, and it would change. Big Webbly and Little Carmen were already feeling the benefits. But those boys and girls who played and danced up a storm each gig? Well, they were still eating grits. Soon, he'd give them a pep talk, take them out for dinner, sweeten the pill until their ships came in. Bigger gigs were coming, with better merchandise on sale, and income from TV. Soon Carmen's "Toreadors" would have mink coats. "Fur coat and no knickers," as Ava said, though he wasn't positive he got her drift. He didn't want any of his performers stuck on grits for long, though, of that he was certain.

Talent was getting free stuff from other places – they were sent clothes and records, instruments, and opportunities to have their pictures taken, and that might keep them sweet a while yet. Yes, one day, some fine day in cinemascope and technicolour, he and Ava would get to pay everyone what they deserved.

"Yes," he said, as whisky circulated his glass, "being Nathan Costain in the here and now's a pretty sweet deal."

He heard Ava's key in the door, seeing edges of pink cashmere wrap and a sharp black point of stiletto-toe.

"I'm your surprise package, Baby," he purred. "And now, I thought we could commence to charm your British public. What do you say?"

Ava, as usual, opened her mouth and uttered something to surprise him completely.

"That's great, Hon," she said, taking off her flamingo-coloured pillbox hat, and carefully placing its pin and grips on the dressing-table top, "but my past's catching up with me in ways I don't like, so we have to watch it. Least you know, more we're better off. Oh, and I think I may have done something to anger Slim du Val, and compromise us."

"Why? Because the fool left us?"

"No. Because I torched his expensive new jacket, and Big Webbly got a communication saying he's going to bad-mouth us, and demand recompense."

"Oh, for the Lawd's sake, Ava, just buy the boy a new jacket."

"It's not as simple as that."

"Why?"

"Big Webbly had this letter from him, and it said Slim'd not cashed-in any of his pay-cheques, and they were all in his jacket pocket. The inside one."

"Well, pay the boy again."

"You know we can't."

"Why's that?"

"Because each time cheques are paid-out, we only just have the money to cover them, after the petrol (you know, "gas"), and publicity, and the stays here, and vans... If our musicians pay their money into the bank, or get cheques cashed when paid, *no problemo*. But if they save them all, then cash them in all at once, they'll bounce."

"Bounce ... as in, we can't cover them?"

"Yeah. Think of it, there's been so much spending. This place doesn't come cheap. Slim's cheques aren't for that much singly, but put them together, you've got one big pay out. I don't think our finances can stand it. Oh, I knew he was a mistake, he's posher than the others, and has family money."

"So, he doesn't need ours."

"No, but he'll take it. Just for spite. And, fair dos, he is owed. Oh, I hate posh boys who don't need cash, they always screw you in some way."

Ava bit her pink-iced lip. "I've boggered it. I'm sorry, Nathan."

Nathan smiled, his widest, most confident smile. "Boggered. That sounds filthy, Ava."

"Sort of."

"Look Darlin'," he said, "we'll do what we always do. Ride it out. I'll contact the dude, let him know what a fool he'll look, keeping his cash in a pocket, like some old dame with her life savings under the bed. And, we only have his word for the fact that's where the money was. I have publicity at my touch he won't want, and if we can't ride it out, then I'll sell my diamond ring. Look, Ava, I didn't come all this way to have a beef about Slim du Val. Screw him. Our popularity's rising now, our ship's damn near in port. Slim du Val? Small fry! Soon we'll be able to pay them all off! Let him wait, they can all wait. Hell, Ava, don't you get it? We're the big noise, Baby – They're working on our time now."

Face to Face

Ava and Nathan had been interviewed on one TV show after another. She was right, everyone loved him, from interviewer to audience. Of course, he was photogenic: "Don't he look like Nat King bloody Cole," as one tea-lady remarked on seeing him enter a building. But they loved him even more when he spoke, those honey-rich tones seemed to talk to you one-on-one. Even when audiences were large, he'd fix on some point in the distance, as though that was the person he *really* wanted to talk to. Or, he'd smile at the interviewer with candour, as if he was giving up a secret to them only. "I'm tellin' this from the heart," he'd laugh, or, "well, as my Daddy used to say…" And he'd have them, then and there, from journalist to sweeper-up, eating out of that well-manicured hand.

"Good job *Face to Face* is no longer on." He said to Ava one night, "I saw an old repeat of one last night, Tony Hancock? Comedian. Boy, I never saw an unhappier guy. Squirming in the chair while that fella Freeman made him confess to all those demons. Man! I almost switched it off."

"I didn't know they were repeating that."

"It was a one-off. Replaced something that was taken off in a hurry."

"You'd've been great, though, Nathan."

"Nah. See, that guy Freeman had a confessional thing goin'. If you noticed, I talk a lot, but seldom give it up. You see, what we're giving them with the tour is pe-zazz, writ large. They don't want to know if my Daddy beat me (which he didn't by the way, even when I fed the neighbour's dog chewin' tobacco), or if I languished for love. They want the sparkle, the everything's OK with us, and it's going to be OK with them, too."

"I see. So, we're big fat liars?"

"Not liars, no, just, well, we're there to shine."

"Nathan, you read it like a book."

And Ava marvelled at Nathan's knowledge of how to work things. He should've looked old fashioned, she knew, in well-cut suits, cashmere coats, tie-pins, and links.   Yet somehow, even beside groups sporting outrageous riding silks, or odd floral blouses, he looked cool.

"The cool of now," thought Ava. She recalled a young man from one of the bands, wearing what looked to her like clashing mulberries and paisleys from his Grandmother's attic, saying, "Great threads, Man" as Nathan walked by. Always, on TV, she knew she was the main course's accompaniment.

Ava also realised, from the way in which conversations, televised or other, latched onto Nathan's every word, that he'd be fine without her.

Something was giving Ava sleepless nights. She loved Nathan, course she did, who wouldn't? But lately, the old need to move on tossed her sheets and made her get up for glass after glass of water, or something stronger. He slept like a heavy statue, always had he said, getting up energetic was his thing. Her wakefulness did not disturb him.

She'd received word from Aggie, a note hand delivered to a TV studio where they were due to appear. She recognised the neat writing on the envelope, before opening it. The letter was on tissue-light paper, and addressed respectfully to "Mrs Ava Costain", but it began with "My dear Gilda" - the very sight of her old name making Ava wince. The whole missive, or so it seemed, was a slap in the face from the past:

My Dear Gilda, Or Ava, if you so prefer.

I almost didn't write this note, but felt I had to. Bin it, burn it, I don't much care about after, but please read it.

And read Ava did, in a toilet at the studio, sitting on the closed seat in her swish get-up, an unfamiliar pricking at the edges of her eyes. She could hear someone humming as they washed their hands, and wished she could go out, wash her hands, and be done with the whole shameful business of ignoring an old friend.

I know, better than anyone, that you had to get away. And think I guessed why, although Phil doesn't know I suspect anything. A few times, a tight-faced little Teddy Boy came to see him from next door, and they huddled in the back room like a pair of nasty old women. That boy doesn't visit now, and Phil seems less jumpy than he did. If I'm right, I don't condone the past, not at all, but we have-to get on with things, don't we?

Since you went, when it became clear you'd gone for good, Phil and I started seeing each other. Comfort on his part, I don't fool myself it's been love's young dream. Besides, he loved you, truly, and I always knew it. We're hitched now, and I hope you don't mind. Oddly enough, we've rubbed-along great.

I haven't told him I saw you at Hannington's, and shan't unless you tell me, face-to-face, you wish it. And, if that day never comes, well, I can just about live with it.'

A prim "PTO", followed by:

So, we're both hitched, and you have carved out a glamorous new life for yourself, as, it seems, have I (without the glamorous, jetting around bit).

And, it's that new life I have-to thank you for, and that's the reason why I'm writing.

Remember, all those years ago, you saved me from the streets? If not for you, I'd be pushing that cart round Brighton's back-alleys, still. Then, Phil found out I'd been a silent movie actress, in the old days.

Well, funny to tell, there's been renewed interest in the silents, lately, those bands in all the weird get-ups, like running old movies behind themselves, and silents are just right for obvious reasons. They say we're adding to the 'counter culture,' though what that means I'm not sure, the counter at Hannington's is far enough for me.

I also keep being asked to speak at events, far afield as the East Midlands!

Well, I was speaking at an East Midlands' do, at a re-opened cinema, and this old woman who organises it (and, in whom I'd confided, without mentioning your name), said: 'You know Love, you're lucky. You got a second go. And how many beggars get to do that in life?'

Another "PTO", then:

To cut my story short, it was then I realised what you'd given me – a second go. At that film night, watching my old self dance and twinkle across the screen, a girl, incidentally, I hardly recognised, it suddenly came to me – you'd saved her, too! Just as that cinema's owner saved his dad's old reels of film.

Gilda, I'm sorry but it seems I can't call you anything else, be happy. Have your life as Mrs Costain, and the hell with what the others think. If you want to see me, fine. But if you don't, I'll not tell Phil, or look for you more.

You might like to know there's an old woman here, I think she was a dancer in a previous life, who I'm intent on saving. So maybe, in the end, you saved three of us, me, the girl on screen, and that old bird I have plans for.

Yours ever, Aggie.

Sweet, sentimental, and honest, everything that Ava decided she wasn't. Her mascara had smudged, she was sure of it. She folded the letter and reached for the inner-pocket of her jacket to put it there. Suddenly, she was aware there was no inner-pocket, that was in the favourite black wool she'd sported during the war. Her finger caught on the raised initials of the expensive jacket's lining. A. C. She smiled, then the thought struck her that once-upon-a-time the initials would have read G. G. She wondered what they'd read a few years hence? It was too late to become settled now.

She rose from the toilet and opened-up the seat. Taking Aggie's letter, she breathed, "Sorry, love," before tearing the three sheets into small fragments and throwing them down the bowl. They'd flush, the paper thin as Izal. She had to do it thrice, but at last the letter was gone. The only evidence it had ever existed was a pale blue ink whirl, circling the water. There might be a blockage, but they'd never know she was culprit. Leaving the cubicle and walking to the mirror, she righted her make-up.

She'd been correct about the mascara, and cleaned up the small dark blodges with a tissue from her hand-bag. A wipe of powder and sprint of lipstick, and she was good to go.

"Jesus, Ava," Nathan said as she emerged, "I thought you'd been abducted, I was about to call the cops."

"Sorry," she said, "last night's dinner didn't agree."

"But I thought you loved trout with almonds?"

"Well, clearly, it doesn't love me."

Walking into the studio with him, she wanted to whisper, "I love you, Nathan Costain." But she didn't, nor did she grasp his fingers in a squeeze. Something in her couldn't stay. Maybe one day, he, like Aggie, would be writing.

They had another interview tomorrow. It would be her last, and perhaps she'd even be a no-show. She'd half-packed two cream Antler cases, one of which, a vanity with peach-silk innards, had cash sewn into the lining. Shameful notes, withdrawn to pay as much of what was owed to Slim du Val as they could afford. She'd steal from Nathan and Slim, in the end. What did anyone expect? With her current dual passport she could travel somewhere else, to another town where she was unknown. Hollywood appealed, some job behind the scenes, who knew? Jet-black hair dye beckoned, and a change of dress. A. C. picked-out, the pale pink suit stained blue.

Nathan would get by.

She was certain.

That smile and *savoir-fare* would get him there.

Meet Your World

Standing in the wings at *New Times Television*, Grandwem and George felt knock-kneed as kids on their first day at school. Grandwem recalled the boy whose fingers were peeled off railings one-by-one, and that feeling of smugness that she was a girl and wasn't letting on like that. Recalled the smell of bottle-green soap, and the teacher (Miss Mobly's) fern perfume. No one would have an old lady perfume like fern, these days, and maybe (thinking of the smell half-way between cut-grass and boiling kale) it was a good thing. Although, having caught the heavy furry notes of Beryl's patchouli oil, she wasn't sure that they were on to such a good thing now, either.

Still, good things were one reason they were here. *Meet Your World* – a show trying to be *This is Your Life*, only on a reduced budget, and without Eamonn Andrews – was about to pay homage to Cooper and Bean.

Grandwem looked around her, also waiting in the wings were Beryl and Ernie, Alf and Shirl and Little Rita. Instead of the famous book there'd be a "file of life" to show Billy and Court. A presenter called Tony (surname that sounded something like "Peas" but probably wasn't) looked a bit like a cut-down Eamonn Andrews, too.

The baby gurgled and clapped, at least she didn't feel on the top-note like Grandwem. A new television station, with them as one of the big opening shows, and the boys suspected nothing! Who'd a thought it?

As they stood, a handsome black man, in an eye-catching cream suit, pushed past them. "Forgive me," he said, with a wide smile Grandwem thought was the saddest she'd ever seen. And what beauteous mohair threads! "Chin up, lovely boy," she said after him, without really knowing why.

Cooper and Bean were on stage in a fund-raiser for London's old halls when the man with the file collared them. They were driven to the studio at speed, audience applause still sounding in their ears. Before they knew it, the set's white glare, and cheers of the new audience assailed them.

"Bloody hell!" hissed Billy, "this is really happening."

*

Nathan Costain had been interviewed in a plush office, smelling of wrappings for furniture, by a studio manager who looked about twelve. He talked of the interview show going out today, and of how *Pop Goes*, the music show, on tomorrow, was their flagship, rivalling anything the Beeb or ITV could turn out. "And the 'groovy' thing is, we're young. 'Happening' as the parlance would have it, we could do anything and the kids would be with us. We know you've been on *Pop It*." Nathan looked at the man's oatmeal sweater, pipe, and heard his Oxbridge intonations. He could be the same manager for any of the television stations. Nathan was supposed to be on screen with Ava tomorrow, and that girl who'd done the pop pictures of them both, based on news cuttings. The pictures would be a back-drop to the whole show.

Despite recent traumas with Ava, Nathan was curious about the girl artist. Ava had really rated her, while papers were full of tales of her hellraising like a fella.

She was one of the last people he and Ava talked about, the night before she left.

"I knew that girl was going to put it about. She's got that sort of face," Ava said, adding, "I bet there's more to bloody come."

In the meeting, Nathan had to think on his feet about reasons why Ava wouldn't be there. Ava had been "unexpectedly called away", he said, and then "more than unavoidably detained". But the note on the dressing-table top back at the hotel room had said nothing so specific.

Dear Nate, it began, *I'm so sorry to do this, in fact, I'm not sure why I am. Truth is, I've always been good at bottling out. I'd like to be nice enough to tell you exactly why I can't carry on with us, but it'd only sound like a crummy excuse. I hope, one day, you'll remember me with affection, and think well of the times we've had. I wish, also one day, you'll find it in yourself not to be too angry that I left. Know you're the best thing that ever happened to me, and I don't leave lightly. Please resist the urge to seek me out, you'll never change my mind,*

Yours ever, Ava.

He'd read that note over and over. Her parting shot, unwanted and unlooked for. It rested in his suit's top-pocket, and he felt as though it were burning the lining.

"God, Ava," he'd whispered, "why'd you need to do that, Baby? Don't ya know I'd've forgiven you anything." But he'd spoken to a dressing-table mirror, in a country he was unfamiliar with, and the person addressed had long gone. And, he knew, had gone for good.

*

"Well, Cooper and Bean, you're more than familiar to our audiences now. Stage, touring, and, of course, small screen. We understand from sources close-by, that there are even toys showing your image. But, it wasn't always like that, was it?"

"Weeell"… Court began.

"No, you were in the services together and invalided out."

"Well…"

"And you had humble beginnings."

"Well, I wouldn't say…"

"That's right."

"You see, how it all began…" Court started again, eager to tell the real story.

"Smashing. Then you found your move to top-billing. And it was big cars all the way for the boys from the humble streets of Nottingham."

"Well, Billy's Nottingham, I'm…"

"Smashing. And now you're gracing telly screens nation-wide."

"Well, we actually reached top stage billing first, years of graft."

"Overnight, though, really."

"You see, we played our way up, you did then, and…"

"But your real success, what you'll be remembered for, is here on the small screen. Maybe you'll even be remembered for tonight, we're a new station, folks!"

Court and Billy realised it was futile to argue the point. They smiled. "Yeah," Billy said, "whichever way you look at it, Court and I have been real lucky."

*

Stella Bax was regarding the giant cut-out of her work in the TV studio, a day prior to the broadcast. She was in a side room, and could hear some show going on elsewhere. Nathan Costain had left the building, she'd been told, thus she'd missed him. Unless he was outside somewhere, introductions would have to wait until tomorrow.

The image was a giant, red-blooded, bloated version of the work she'd first come-up with. She thought of her Dad, sitting in his unchanged living room, snorting at a pop programme. Maybe he'd see it, and her? But no, first strains and he'd click-over to something more familiar. "Bloody long haired louts, and the girls, slags to a woman."

Opening her white leather, Mary Quant bag, with its daisy clasp, she reached for her lip-gloss in its yellow and orange container. The art piece didn't look right, it was too big, too blotchy. But thousands would see it, and her. She needed a drink, a gin with something. Reaching again into the bag, she felt for the hip-flask covered in psychedelic paisley fabric. "Shit." She breathed, thinking how her Dad hated women using "language".

Tomorrow, she would hold Mr Costain's hand if she could – she was that nervous.

Plus, she'd received note from Mrs Costain, written on hotel paper and waiting for her at the TV studio when she arrived.

Dear Miss Bax, or Stella, or artist about to make it big, this began, *I'm sorry our acquaintance won't be longer. I shall follow your work with interest, but doubt if we'll see each other again. If you recognise me somewhere in the future, it will no doubt be a me with a different name and appearance. I'd appreciate it if you seem never to have met me before. Speaking of which, please, try not to look surprised when Nathan lies about my whereabouts on-screen tomorrow, truth is I've left him for good, and his world of music on the never-never.*

Tomorrow will be hard for him, so please be kind, as the song goes. I'm as proud of your work as your Ma would have been – I doubt we'll meet again, but if I had a daughter, I'd want her to turn-out like you.

So, my dear, good luck, don't party too hard, and keep going, love, Ava Costain.

If Stella could have but known it, in Brighton, Aggie was reading a similar letter, though without the art and pride bits. Ava telling her Gilda was no more, and Ava was no more, and it was doubtful that their eventful paths would cross again. It was a letter Ava had surprised herself by writing. Life was hard, Aggie thought, but at least she had Phil, and wasn't saddled with a violent little sod like Ivy's Ted.

Stella Bax took a swig from the paisley and neon flask. "I wish you had been my mum," she breathed, "maybe I wouldn't be in this mess; now they know me as much for behaving badly as for art, they're waiting for it. I can't stop, Ava. Never could."

During her career, Stella would paint Mrs Costain again and again, totemic figure in pale suit, cream hat, and sunglasses that shaded an indistinct face with palely glossed lips. The image would never be satisfactory, and never enough.

*

The introductions had been made, the audience eased in, and the presenter's smile had flashed like a pair of giant dentures. The producers hadn't let Grandwem bring George Formby or Peggy the owl, which she was sorry about. "We can't entertain livestock, Mrs Bean, it's against studio policy."

"A budgie en't livestock, he's family, like the owl. You wouldn't understand, young man, more's the pity."

"Well, even so, we're not equipped."

"I'm not askin' you to build a pen or arena! I could just bring George in his cage, and Peggy sits on Alf's arm lovely."

"It wouldn't be suitable."

"They're more house-trained than you, but fair enough." Grandwem had given in, whilst privately thinking there was no telling some folk, a budgie and an owl would be great TV.

Standing in the wings waiting for your turn to go on, made you think back over the years all right. The boys were lucky, it was true, but at a price. Ruby had left Billy again, and the son he didn't know he had was at her Majesty's. Neither Bill nor Court were happily hitched like Morecambe and Wise, and Court hadn't found a 'Miss Right' since Vi. One thing was gladdening, she thought, their Beryl seemed settled with Ernie and had always seemed to see her teenage crush on Court for what it was.

If only Rita could be with them now, and Norrie, standing back-stage, or whatever you called the telly's nethers. They could share this with Rita and her last brother, Grandwem mused, Rita in her best plum-velvet frock, and Norrie all scrubbed-up in neckerchief and moleskin trousers. He'd've made them have the owl, and some terriers besides! He'd have even taken the string and bike clips from his ensemble. As if he was going to the wrestling with those hopeful old biddies, who used to collect him on a Saturday night.

Grandwem's reverie was broken by a young woman in a frightening shade of orange lipstick, who said it was their turn. "You're on," she snorted, checking her clip-board. "I'm here to lead you through." Grandwem grabbed George's fingers. "Me combinations don't feel straight."

"You always say that before the film comes on at Birch's," he said, "but they always bleddy are."

*

Outside, Nathan Costain threw the last of his cigarette onto the ground. Things were as they were, and he'd have to do without Ava. He knew it. Seated on a low wall, he looked around him, wondering why so many vistas looked the same. The swing doors made their swishing noise, and a young woman in a floral swirled dress walked from the building. Her handbag was patterned with daisies. She came up to him and gave him a broad smile, that Nathan thought the saddest he'd ever seen.

"Hi, Mr Costain. I'm Stella Bax, the artist, and I'm sorry about Ava. She wrote and told me she was going." Miss Bax dug in the bag, and produced a hip-flask of many colours. "Gin. From my experience, I find it helps," she said.

*

210

In the studio, everything was all lights and noise. Sitting before Grandwem and the family, Courtney and Billy looked happy, smart, and agitated. The crowd sounded like it was at Saturday football, cheering on The Stags.

"Well," the man with the file was saying, "Mr Cooper, how do you really think you and Billy got to be here? Now, at the top of your game?"

"Oh," said Courtney, beaming, "that's simple. We had support, see? Like people you've known since you were a nipper, that connection money can't buy. You think you're talking to a star? You're not. You're talking to a performer. Being a sentimental old fool, let me introduce you to a *real* star – Grandwem. Take a bow!"